ADVANCE PI
AS SUMMER'S MASK SLIPS
AND OTHER DISRUPTIONS

Gordon B. White's stories are weird and wise and always surprising. An impressive first collection.

—Kij Johnson,
author of *The Dream-Quest of Vellitt Boe*

Tapping into the atmosphere, authority, and history of Southern gothic fiction, Gordon B. White's collection of horror stories is haunting, lyrical, and unsettling. There is a primal fear that lurks in us all: a worry that just beyond the end of the flashlight beam waits unimaginable horror—and this cornucopia of dark tales proves that point.

—Richard Thomas,
author of *Disintegration* and the Thriller-nominated *Breaker*

White's stories fly up, weird embers bright and true.

—Adam Golaski,
author of *Worse Than Myself* and *Color Plates*

Gordon B. White's range is as broad as his humanity is deep. From nightmarish drainage problems that bring out the best a father can be, to back-county vengeance that pushes the boundaries of extended family, White is always a romantic, albeit an abyssal one. He weirds the dystopian and transforms the familiar—his prose is in turns eerie and elegant and often both, reaching into the darkness, as one of his characters says, from which anything could emerge. In these tales it does.

—J.S. Breukelaar,
author of *Collision: Stories*

The catchy cadences of Gordon B. White's prose serve as stepping stones for readers crossing the pleasantly deceptive arteries of his disquieting narratives. *As Summer's Mask Slips and Other Disruptions* is an impressive exercise in precision, and a celebration of the unsettling.

—Clint Smith,
author of *Ghouljaw and Other Stories* and *The Skeleton Melodies*

Smart, spooky, and heartfelt. Gordon B. White's stories for readers who like their tales weird and full of solid storytelling.

—Daniel Braum,
author of *The Night Marchers and Other Strange Tales*

These stories are full of gritty magic, dark imagination, and a whole choir of storytelling voices, each with their own unsettling precision. Gordon will have you grinding your teeth as he pulls you through the ventricles of your own heart.

—Sarah Read,
author of *The Bone Weaver's Orchard* and *Out of Water*

With his debut collection, Gordon B. White establishes himself as one of the major new voices of speculative fiction. A quiet creeping dread that never lets up, *As Summer's Mask Slips and Other Disruptions* explores pain, loneliness, and horror through a deeply personal lens of family and outsiders. These unforgettable short stories are not to be missed.

—Gwendolyn Kiste,
Bram Stoker Award®-winning author of *The Rust Maidens*

As Summer's Mask Slips is an impressive debut for Gordon B. White. The stories herein are imbued with a rough grace; there's an earthy layer of very human grit present for the supernatural elements to rub against, resulting in narratives that shine in the darkness. From backwoods steeped in dusty occult ritual to the kinetic free-for-all of a bleak dystopia, White demonstrates an elegant ability to craft stories with heart and soul at the core of the horror. A brilliant, highly recommended collection.

—Scott R. Jones,
author of *Shout Kill Revel Repeat* and *Stonefish*

AS SUMMER'S MASK SLIPS

AND OTHER DISRUPTIONS

GORDON B. WHITE

TREPIDATIO
PUBLISHING

ISBN: 978-1-950305-20-9 (sc)
ISBN: 978-1-950305-21-6 (ebook)
Library of Congress Control Number: 2019953120

First printing edition: January 31, 2020
Printed by Trepidatio Publishing in the United States of America.
Cover Design and Layout: Don Noble / Rooster Republic Press
Interior Layout: Lori Michelle
Edited by Scarlett R. Algee
Proofread by Sean Leonard

Trepidatio Publishing, an imprint of JournalStone Publishing
3205 Sassafras Trail
Carbondale, Illinois 62901

Trepidatio books may be ordered through booksellers or by
contacting:
Trepidatio | www.trepidatio.com
or
JournalStone | www.journalstone.com

PUBLICATION HISTORY

"As Summer's Mask Slips." *Nightscript* Volume 2, ed. C.M. Muller, 2016.

"Birds of Passage." *Twice-Told: A Collection of Doubles*, ed. C.M. Muller, 2019. Reprinted at *Pseudopod*, ed. Shawn Garrett & Alex Hofelich, 2019.

"The Buchanan Boys Ride Again." *Creatures: Novelette Edition*, ed. Andrea Dawn, 2019.

"Clara Walker's Little Death." *Dark Moon Digest* No. 24, ed. Lori Michelle, 2016.

"Eight Affirmations for the Revolting Body, Confiscated from the Prisoners of Bunk 17." *Not One of Us* No. 61, ed. John Benson, 2019.

"Hair Shirt Drag." *Wrapped in Black: 13 Tales of Witches & the Occult*, ed. Jennifer L. Greene, 2014. Reprinted in *We Are Not This: Carolina Writers for Equality*, ed. John G. Hartness, Melissa Gilbert, & Jay Requard, 2016.

"The Hollow." *Dark Fuse - Horror D'oeuvres*, ed. Shane Staley, 2014.

"The Lure of the Lollipop Tree." (original to this publication)

"The Meatbag Variations." (original to this publication)

"Mise en Abyme." *Borderlands* No. 6, ed. Tom Monteleone and Olivia Monteleone, 2016.

"Open Fight Night at the Dirtbag Casino." *A Breath from the Sky: Unusual Stories of Possession*, ed. Scott R. Jones, 2017.

"The Rising Son." *Cease, Cows*, ed. H.L. Nelson, 2013.

"The Sputtering Wick of the Stars." *Halloween Forevermore*, ed. Terry M. West, 2015.

"Ultramarine." *Lakeside Circus*, ed. Carrie Cuinn, 2014.

"We Eat Dirt and Sleep and Wait." *Tales to Terrify*, ed. Scott Silk, 2019.

TABLE OF CONTENTS

For my father, James—a teller of tall tales and gone too soon.

AS SUMMER'S MASK SLIPS
AND OTHER DISRUPTIONS

INTRODUCTION

I'**M OFTEN MET WITH A** smile when people hear that I'm a writer. I can predict—almost to the second—how long the smile will last, because the inevitable question that follows is, "What do you write?"

"Horror." I used to dance around a bit and splash some condiments on the word. *Dark fiction. Occult.* Now it's just, "Horror."

"Oh," they reply, as if unsure of their social obligation to continue the conversation. But like a kid peeking through fingers, they're compelled to offer an opinion before fleeing.

"That's so *weird.*"

I hasten to explain that horror writers are normal people. At any literary convention you'll see groups of writers peeling off by genre, invariably the horror writers are at the bar, or gathered in a hotel room to swap stories over a bottle of Scotch. They wear t-shirts and sports jackets and jeans like anyone else. They eat pizza and lobster rolls and . . .

It doesn't work. My words bounce off the shield of their preconceptions.

I used to worry about it.

I first met Gordon White at a writer's convention. Fit, friendly and open-faced, you'd never peg him as a horror writer. I remember sitting down in the hotel bar for a beer to talk with a guy in the early stages of his writing career. He was already a husband and a lawyer, already writing book reviews, but I wasn't imagining his first book at that meeting. I'm not sure he was either.

A first book is a helluva thing. The world wants to kill it. Picture baby sea turtles breaking out their eggs and scuttling across the open sand towards the water, set upon by seagulls and crabs and even the surf itself until only a small percentage makes it to the open sea.

First books are like that. Many are conceived. Few are completed. Fewer still are published.

As Summer's Mask Slips and Other Disruptions is Gordon's first book, and that's a helluva thing.

It's also a helluva good book.

It's dark as I write this, a chilly October evening with a smattering of rain. Appropriate weather, in other words. It's what we expect when we talk about horror.

Gordon doesn't write about what's expected. He writes about the mask slipping. The unsettling truth behind the smile. Behind *his* smile, perhaps.

Gordon's language is literary—in the most complimentary sense of the word—and his stories carry power. I imagine Joyce Carol Oates turning her talent towards a tale with the grit of a pulp. Most writers will land on one side or the other of that prose divide, but Gordon's unique voice blends the styles together seamlessly. He's a city guy who used to live in New York City and now makes his home in Seattle, but many of his stories are placed in remote, rural locales where the peace and quiet promises safety. There's a particular kind of fear to be found in a lonely house out in the woods once you peel away the mask. You won't find the barrier between realities thinning as you walk down Fifth Avenue, but you might find it if you canoe far enough down river that you've left all traces of roads and houses and humanity behind. Some things find it easier to grow unmolested in isolation and it's the foolish person who ventures into those places.

Like I said, however, Gordon is a city guy and understands the isolation that can occur in the midst of a crowd. The striving of an artist who can't express her yearning through a language that anyone else will understand. The march of a prizefighter before a howling crowd in the bleachers. In its own way this isolation, this internal darkness, provides a safe place for strange, dark things to grow until they are strong enough to tear aside the tissue-thin veneer of civilization and make themselves known.

INTRODUCTION

There are fifteen tales in this collection, the stories as varied as the terrors they explore, and I'd like to provide a few signposts for those of you about to dive in. Just a few, though. Any more would be cheating.

Charging out of the gate like a racehorse, *Hair Shirt Drag* gives us a coming of age tale that revels in power unleashed, a clarion call for the misunderstood. But silence can be as threatening as a roar, and Gordon lowers his voice to lure readers close with *Ultramarine*, where isolated beauty promises respite and offers something else entirely. In *The Meatbag Variations*, Gordon shows his quiet powers of observation as an artist struggling for perfection finds it in her doppelganger. A unique story, possibly the most unique story in the entire book. I've never read its like.

Fear is approached from a different angle in the final story, *Birds of Passage*, as a father takes his son on a camping trip to experience something he can barely describe. "It's a soft place, I think. It isn't quite here, and isn't quite there. There aren't roads, but you can feel that something more surrounds us." Gordon has taken us on a journey into The Weird as deftly and delicately as a maestro, and it's a fitting choice to close this volume, because it will stay with you. It stayed with me.

The inviting elegance of the writing in these stories reminds me of the author himself, as if the nature of both man and word is a lure. A trap. There are witches in these pages. There are night skies devoid of stars. There is human cruelty, the dangerous lure of nature and the terrifying disregard of cosmic powers.

It takes time for writers—most writers—to develop a clear voice, but Gordon's voice is as clear as a bell. A first book is a helluva thing and *As Summer's Mask Slips and Other Disruptions* is no exception. It doesn't matter if it's raining where you are or if the sun is shining brightly, turn the page and the mask will slip. The road ahead is dangerous, but I think you'll agree that it's worth the journey.

John C. Foster
Brooklyn, NY
October 12, 2019

HAIR SHIRT DRAG

IAIN'T NEVER READ THE *Key of Solomon*, but I read the Book of Kings. Rest of the Bible, too, back when Mama thought that'd help me fit in. It didn't, I won't, and, truth be told, I ain't all that broken up about it. It's hard being the only son in a family of powerful women, harder still when people say you don't even rate as man enough for that. But I'm just about over it all, really.

It's a humid evening in *Ju-ly*, as Mama says, accenting both syllables. We're on the porch, listening to the crickets and the frogs settle into their nightly delirium as fireflies rise up across the tobacco fields like ghost lights. Mama's got a mouthful of needles as she helps me pin the dress I'm wearing. She ain't thrilled to be doing it, but I need help on the back, and at least out here the cicadas drown out her disapproving clucks.

An engine rattling across the field and a red dust cloud barreling down the driveway interrupt our work. It ain't even really dark yet, but the car's headlights are beaming like two wide eyes scared that something's going to jump out at them. As it gets closer, I recognize Emma Turner, a girl I knew from school and the kind that shakes her long blonde hair when she gets out of her car like this is a shampoo commercial. Almost without thinking, I brush my hand across the nearly-shaved side of my own head, bristling out a fine mist of sweat. I'm not petty or anything, but she and I have never gotten along.

"Evening, Ms. Overhold," she says to Mama.

Mama nods. "It is."

Emma's mouth hangs open as she hesitates, deciding how to address me.

See, Overhold is a matrilineal name, passed on through our family's women, although I ended up with that gift, too, despite my sex. Which was fine, until I got to Bushrod Johnson High and the kids all started calling me "Sissy," but since that's a diminutive—sometimes even an affectionate—of names like Melissa or Jesse, I could pretend it wasn't all that bad. You know, if you squinted hard enough. Anyway, I never let it give them power over me because if there's one thing I know, it's this: Words don't mean nothing. It's only intention that makes things happen.

That's important.

"Jesse." Emma settles on my boy name, smiling as if she and I were on speaking terms. "You're looking thin."

Her eyes laugh the way her mouth wouldn't dare in front of Mama. I must look a mess, hair frizzed out and make-up smearing in the damp air, probably more than a little five o'clock shadow. But girls like Emma eat weakness, so I lean in and smile back.

"You, too, Goldie." The nickname sounds innocuous, but she and I both know the rumors behind it.

Her smile hardens and she shakes her hair again, probably not even meaning to, yet ruled by an instinctual vanity. She tugs at her curls, a tell she's had since middle school when lying to teachers or her boyfriend Tommy Stinz. "I like your," her free hand waves, "get-up. Trash chic."

Half made-up though I may be, I look good in this dress. The sharp lines, cutouts, sloping hem and everything else is my design and my construction. So if queen bee wants to start pulling on threads, jealous that I look better than she ever will, well, that won't end nicely. I sweep the longer part of my hair out of my eyes to stare at her.

"How's your family, Miss Turner?" Mama is louder than the question warrants, pushing herself into the conversation. "Your mother and the sheriff doing well?"

I'm over it. I let go of the moisture-swollen railing, peeled paint stuck beneath my nails. It's too hot for this nonsense.

"Yes, ma'am," Emma says. Her smile is as thin and painted on as her eyebrows, but she sounds sweet as honey.

HAIR SHIRT DRAG

"That's good to hear." Mama hands me my pincushion and waves Emma onto the porch. "What can we do for you?"

"Well, ma'am," Emma says, "I been told to come ask about your medicine."

Now, we call it medicine, but that's just a name to hide behind. Mostly it's little things: minor healing, divination, a love spell or two. But sometimes it's big medicine: the kind that you probably go your whole life never needing, but when you do, you need it more than anything and there's just one place to get it. The Overhold women can do it. I can, too, even though I probably shouldn't be able to.

Emma sits down as Mama picks up a ball of beeswax from the porch railing and pulls out the pieces of straw that run through it. Then Mama rolls the ball between her palms, reforming it like it was never any different than the way she wants it now.

"Tell me," Mama says, beginning the patter I've heard a thousand times. "Have you ever had your future told?" In Emma's eyes, I see her little mind wrestling between wanting to believe and needing to doubt.

"Angels got their wings," Mama goes on. "But I got my ball of wax. You just pick a piece of straw from that broom there and I'll push it through, bending and crossing, twisting and turning. We call it riding the broom, but it's just following the path and reading the passage. Ain't none of us can fly, but this is like seeing everything from above."

I'm over this, too.

Back inside the house, I let the screen door slam and Gatty, our dog, comes into the kitchen. She cocks her head at that angle that dogs do so well and I bend down, take her ears in my hands and rub our faces together. That warm dog smell surrounds me as I tease the fluff on the sides of her neck.

"Why don't you go keep an eye on Mama, girl?"

Gatty shakes out from tip to tail, then trots over and noses the screen open. I can rest a little easier, but the house isn't any cooler than outside and there's no chance for a breeze, so I head towards the back. It's straight through the kitchen and the living room, where we got a fireplace we never use on account of the TV's giant silver ears only get reception right in front of it. Above the fireplace, though, is a photograph of Great-grandma Charity, still smiling down over her house, every bit the proud Overhold matron. I never knew her, but Grandma said that Charity's hair was the silver of thermometer mercury, and that in the moonlight you could see her moving like a star across the fields. It must have been too bright for the black and white film, though, because the crown of her head seems to fan out and disappear into the photo's borders.

Although this house was a tight fit when it was Grandma, Mama, and me, it's a bit more tolerable ever since Grandma passed. With those two taking turns trying to scare me straight with the fear of Jesus while still learning me the Overhold women's medicine, I didn't get a moment's peace. I would lie here on the foldout at night and stare up at Charity shining like a blown-out star and think how things might be different if she were still around. Sometimes I'd fall asleep and dream of her whispering secrets to me and holding my hand, smiling all the while.

You see, Charity got this house and this land from the Beltair family when old Ms. Beltair had a sickness no doctor nor preacher could cure. Finally, Mr. Beltair, with his wife shrunk to skin and bones, went out into the woods where Charity lived with her daughter, my grandma. Mr. Beltair asked her real nice—you didn't ask Charity any way but real nice—to come and use her powers, but she just laughed and said she didn't have no powers, only the medicine. But, like I always say, the words ain't the important bit.

When she got there, the Beltair house was on the edge of mourning. The roosters had been taken away and thick linen sheets sat next to every mirror. But Charity told the men there wasn't nothing to fear just yet. They took her to the sick woman's bedside, and Charity had a long, loud conversation with the airs around her as Ms. Beltair shook and moaned. Then, fast as you please, Charity plucked a mouse from out of the sick woman's forehead, put it in a mason jar, took it home and buried it at the edge of the woods. Grandma used to say that mouse was the sorriest-looking thing she'd ever laid eyes on and sometimes, at night, she used to imagine that she could still hear it tapping against the glass underground.

HAIR SHIRT DRAG

Two days later the Beltair woman was out of bed, and the day after that, the Overhold women were in this house. It was smaller then, a sharecropper's shack that's now the living room that we've built up around, but Charity's portrait still watches over its old heart. Nowadays, though, nobody knows Beltair but as the name on the road that connects the interstate to the bypass, but Grandma's in the churchyard, Charity's in the plot out back, Mama's on the porch, and I'm here in between.

I blow a kiss to Charity as I step out onto the back porch, where I can still hear Mama and Emma on the other side, oohing and ahhing, riding that broom. It's a ridiculous name and, frankly, a ridiculous method. There's plenty of other ways to do it. For example, Gypsy girls use cards and balls. English ladies look at tea leaves. I tried that once, when I was working the dinner shift at the Pig-Heaven-Q, cleaning out a five-gallon cooler of sweet tea dregs and watching this whole town's future spin down the drain of an industrial sink. That was enough for me. Nowadays, I find the best way to learn things is just to ask the right person.

Gatty comes running around the house and jumps up, pawing at my bare legs. I bend down and scratch her chin to calm her.

"What is it, girl?"

She whines and whimpers.

"I see. Well, then." I rub her down real quick, shedding tufts of fluff into the thick air, and then she walks off.

I walk past the fenced-in garden, where there's a pumpkin growing that literally has Ms. Cherise's daughter's name on it. It's growing well and, right on schedule, Ms. Cherise has got a grandbaby due in November, just so long as I get this one up before the frost comes. But straws, pumpkins, balls of wax—these are all props and misdirection. They ain't the power itself, and they don't control the outcome. For instance, Grandma healed plantar warts by laying on hands and speaking in tongues. Mama does it while she rubs your heel and says the Lord's Prayer. Last time I did it was by giving Tommy Stinz a handjob in the locker room while humming "Smells Like Teen Spirit." Sure, gym class was a little awkward after that, but all three of us had one hundred percent success rates and repeat customers.

All that, though, is still easy medicine. Broomsticks, warts, talking dogs, changeling gourds—that's just toying with intent. Something bigger is on the horizon, but it's a dark shape whose edges I can't quite see. I ponder this as I head towards the small gravestones at the woods' edge.

———

Mama and I are sitting at the table after a mostly silent dinner when she looks at me real serious. "Jesse." She starts with my name, which is never a good omen. "We have to do some big medicine."

"For that girl who came by today?" I push my chair back to stand. "Uh-uh. That bitch—"

"Boy, you watch your language. You think your great-grandma would have tolerated that in this house?"

From my seat, I see Charity smiling back at me. "She never complained before."

"Boy," Mama says, and I can tell that I shouldn't push her, because she's always in a foul mood when she starts harping on my sex. "You're awfully presumptuous. Do you think you know her?"

I could push the issue, but I'm over it. "No, ma'am." I settle down into my chair, waiting to follow Mama's lead.

She smoothes the front of her blouse and adjusts the pins holding back her auburn hair. Queen of the house, primping to deliver her address.

"Now, like I said," she finally says, "we're going to have to do the rites."

"What rites?"

She ignores me, standing instead to clear the dishes, so I do the same and follow her into the kitchen. I watch her reflection in the window over the sink as she sets to washing them, scowling down at her busy hands and speaking to the wall.

"It takes a lot of work, because of the gifts we got, to be accepted in this community. We keep hold over the medicine, but it hasn't always been easy." She puts her dishes in the drying rack and takes mine from me, making eye contact for just a second before turning away. "You see, each Overhold woman—well, each Overhold—has got to undertake a certain rite of passage and protection. It helps us and it helps the town."

Her voice is that tired timbre on the verge of cracking that I remember hearing say 'Why can't you be normal?' more times than I'd like to count. It doesn't make me inclined to listen.

"This town can screw," I say.

Dishwater droplets burst like stars as Mama slaps me, hard. My hand goes to my face and my eyes are watering and I don't know whether to laugh or cry or take her head off.

"Oh, baby," she says, like it suddenly hit her too. "I'm so sorry." Her hands are cool and wet from the dishwater against my burning cheek, but I pull back. I've heard these words before, seen these gestures, and I'm over it.

"You can't ever talk that way." She reaches for my arm as I back into the living room. "You have to appreciate what the folks have done for us. You have to do this for them. For us."

My fire is gone, but the anger is changing its shape, becoming something tall and dark.

"Why? Ever since I was born, nobody here has ever made me welcome."

"That's not true, honey." She uses that placating tone usually reserved for Emma and the others that come asking for help. "They let us live here."

"What do you mean?" I pull my arm from her, sweeping it to encompass the room and Great-grandma Charity looking down. "This is our house. We don't owe any rent, we don't need permission."

A strand of Mama's hair has come loose and hangs across her face like a scar, splitting her in two. She pushes it back and, in the same slow gesture, points to the faded portrait of my great-grandma— Mama's grandma—with the bright eyes and halo of quicksilver hair bleeding out into the over-exposure.

"Do you see the way your great-grandma Charity is smiling? How her eyes are wide open, watching us?"

I nod.

"But they ain't quite straight, are they? Her left eye is looking over here at the sofa, but the right, maybe a little, is looking at the table?"

I hadn't ever put my finger on it, but I can't not see it now. Her smile, too, looks off, pulled up not quite at the corners. I look to Mama and realize she's watching me.

"And the way her hair is almost floating? Spilling out like she was underwater, or maybe lying down? Why do you think that is?"

I think I know now, but I don't want to.

"She's dead there, Jesse. Your grandma, my mama, and me had to lay her out, roll her eyes back and stitch her lips together." Her voice swells with righteous air. "Do you know why you don't see Beltairs around here? For the same reason you don't see your great-grandma. It's because Mr. Beltair gave Charity this house, called it a gift, but one day his sons came and told Charity and your grandma to leave. Charity asked them, 'Don't your daddy's word mean nothing?' And they laughed and said words are just words.

"Well, she should have just said all right and left, but there never was a woman less aptly named than your great-grandma. So she worked her medicine and, after that, what Beltairs weren't dead surely wished they were. But when the rest of the town found out, they came here, all of them. And they would have been right, wouldn't they, to have dragged them both out into the woods and burned them to ashes. But they didn't. Instead, when they were done with Charity, just Charity, they said to your grandma, 'We did you this kindness, so you're gonna do us the same.'

"So you be thankful that they let your grandma and me live here, let us shop in their town, join their church. That they let us bury your grandma in the churchyard and not in a hole out back. That they let you and me go to their school and talk to their children, and if you didn't fit in, that's not anyone's fault but your own for insisting on being so damn," she spits the word like a curse, "*odd*."

And so the night has led back to the place where it always leads.

"All the Overhold women have daughters, so when you were born I hoped, prayed, that the line was broken and that you wouldn't have the gifts, but you did. And I don't know why, even being a boy, you can't just be a real one. It's like you try to undo all of our work, but I won't let you. You have got to do this now, for me, whether you want to or not."

I'm over it. My mind is a place of shadows until I realize that Mama is now standing before me.

"Jesse, honey." The huckster voice is back. "Will you do this, please?"

I'm tired of fighting it, so I give in and nod.

"Good," she says. "That's real good."

<hr />

From inside her closet, Mama pulls out a large fur coat, but as it comes into the light, I can see that it isn't an animal's skin. At least not one animal's. It's a patchwork of fur and hair, different colors, different patterns, different lengths. As I look at it, it seems less and less like a coat and more and more like a ball of beasts all stitched together.

"Do you know what this is?" Mama lays it down gently on the bed, like she's afraid something's going to break or, maybe, fall out.

"Clearly," I say, "it's a Bigfoot costume."

Mama laughs, an unfamiliar sound. "That's one name it's gone by."

Static, maybe, crackles as her fingers run furrows through the pelts and the smell of musk and something sweet, like honeysuckle, sneaks into the room. She smiles in a way I've never seen.

"There's power in the flesh; in the hair and skin. That's old medicine, blood medicine. We don't do that anymore." She trembles slightly, her fingers clenching. "But this has been in our family since before we had a name. Across the seas, they called it a hair shirt, and it made them closer to God. In the swamps, when women who wore it ran like wolves, they called it *loup garou.*"

I see now that there's not a rabbit fur nor deerskin among the pieces. These are hunters: a bear's coat, a wolf's hide, a few patches I can't guess, and more than a few long, lanky ones that I can, but don't want to.

"Generation by generation, my family"—she frowns—"*our* family, added to it. It grew longer and longer, covering more and more. Size of a bobcat, size of a bear, size of a skunk ape."

"And what does it do?" I speak softly, cowed by the only half-ridiculous fear that I might somehow wake it up.

"It makes the medicine stronger." She lets go slowly, letting the hair run through her fingers like sand.

"And you use this in the ceremony?"

"No, baby, you do."

As my hands near the coat, the air between us is writhing. There's heat and pulse, whispers and growls, dark paws and bare feet on the forest floor. But when I pick it up, it's so light that it's almost rising up to meet me, clinging to my hands.

"Do you feel it?" Mama asks.

"Yes, ma'am."

"Be very careful with it."

The misshapen bulk looms before me, an untamed bramble of dark medicine. I can see the potential, but it's going to need some alterations.

A week later, when the full moon rises, Mama stands in a clearing that's painted red and orange by a singing bonfire. Hidden in the tree line, I watch the ritual as I dress in my second skin. Fireflies blink like curious eyes, but I feel amazing and have no shame in this form. The changes I've made to the hair shirt were extreme, but no matter how much I trimmed, tightened, and realigned, I didn't end up with any more or less than I started with. It was like we were working together towards a mutual design. Anyway, I look damn good.

In the semi-circle of seven or eight spectators watching Mama and the fire, I recognize Emma's golden hair, even in the dark. The others are a mystery, since it was hard enough to get Mama to tell me the purpose of this ceremony, much less who's here. She was vague, but it's some sort of protection rite to reinforce the boundaries of the town. Every generation, a group of them comes to us for the medicine—the big medicine—and the next generation of Overhold women obliges them with a show of power. It's like a black mass cotillion, I guess. From what Gatty said, I'd had my misgivings, but right now I'm too excited by the feel of the shadows and the breeze

HAIR SHIRT DRAG

running through the hairs on my head and the ones on my ceremonial dress, drawing goose bumps where they brush against my naked arms and thighs. I'm a stunning weeping willow made of darkness, just waiting for my cue.

For once, Mama isn't chanting the Lord's Prayer, but a full-on incantation. The fire twists and cackles, driving back the spectators and their shadows. The flame bursts and here I go.

I strut out into the light and I own this forest. Each step drives like a root into the ground, sending out shockwaves as the night trembles before me. At the fire's edge I see Mama's mouth gaping. The hair shirt isn't a lumpy bear costume anymore, but pure totemic fetish. If she was expecting that homeless Sasquatch look, then this high-fashion fur drag priestess must be blowing her mind. Everyone is speechless.

Short skirt, plunging neckline, thigh-highs and arm bangles all positively coursing with power. The red lips and smoky eye aren't medicine, but they might as well be magic. I plant myself by the fire, hips cocked and arms akimbo to let them finally look upon my realness.

For a moment, there are no words.

"Sissy?" Emma is the first to break the spell, forgetting to use my boy name in front of Mama.

"Holy moly." That's Tommy Stinz, with the same stunned look I remember from the locker room.

But that was the preview, and now here comes the show. The power courses down from the sky and up from the forest floor, through the dark hairs that stretch outwards, grasping like antennae. All around me, the black begins to take solid form as the strength of the beasts and men that I am wearing bends around me. I have wings of night and stars, claws of purest void, and I feel like I could reach through the canopy and pluck down the silver moon.

"Abracadabra, bitches."

But then I am smashed out of my triumph, screaming as something long and heavy whips across my back. I scream and break under the blows.

"Get him," someone shouts. All around, flashlights flare like

11

angry stars and I hear footsteps and more voices, older voices, coming out of the trees and into the clearing. I can only make out their silhouettes behind the fire, but it seems like the whole town is here, watching as the thick chain is wrapped around my throat and arms, pulling and spreading me like a deer on a car's hood. It's heavy and cold, and my skins recoil beneath its touch.

I recognize Sheriff Turner, Emma's daddy, by his uniform. He grabs the hair on my head and pulls it back, lifting my face to the assembly.

"Iron binds the witch," he says.

"Amen," the crowd responds.

Sheriff Turner keeps talking, but the frozen weight of my bindings and the links biting into my bare skin are too much. Rolling my eyes, I see Mama standing off to the side of the group. Her face looks like it's burning the same color as her hair. She looks away when she sees me watching her.

"Witches have power, but together we are as strong as iron. Come up here." The sheriff gestures to Emma and the others. "It ain't nothing to be scared of."

One by one, they are buoyed up by the rest of the town's whispering approval. A girl and a boy I can't place are first, and they poke me in the chest, push me back. The chains dig in, and I can feel the skin beginning to tear.

Emma comes next and her father pulls my head up so that I can face her as she slaps me, lightly first, then much harder.

"That's enough," he says, but he doesn't sound convinced. She gets one more in.

Then comes Tommy Stinz, and I'm afraid he going to punch me, but instead he leans in close and, for a split second, I think maybe he's going to kiss me, but he just spits out an insult. "Freak." Then he gets right next to my ear and I can feel the tingle of his breath as he calls me the other f-word. At that point, I begin to cry.

A parade of horribles goes by, laughing and spitting, pinching and prodding. They run together like mascara, but through my tears I recognize the last one by her tight red hair.

"Mama?"

"I'm sorry," she says. "But we all have to do this. This is how you learn what it means to be a part of the community."

She turns her back and, just like that, I'm over it. Really, truly over it.

The power gathers to me, iron chains be damned, and when I hear Mama gasp, I know she now sees the other alteration I've made to this dress. Like beams of moonlight, the braids of quicksilver trim that I've added begin to tremble, and there's more anger here than just mine.

"Charity?" Mama whispers.

The sheriff's grip tightens, but I just laugh. "Not on your life."

And then I explode. The iron chain shatters, links tearing through my captors like shrapnel. Sheriff Turner staggers backwards, reaching for his holster, but I'm that dark place where the shadows move, and it ain't safe to be near me. Unseen hands reach through and into him, stopping his heart. The silver strands of my war dress sparkle like razor wires, and I close my eyes to finally reveal the second set of black ones I've painted on the lids. Dark eyes, dark hair swirling into the shadows. I am the negative portrait of Charity as I finish her work.

The bonfire erupts into the crowd, sending screaming matchstick men and women into the trees, carrying the flames like my emissaries. All around, I swing my long dark arms of night, crashing through wood and bone, stone and flesh. Those that don't break are bent and twisted into wrongful, knotted things.

I hone in on Emma's golden crown and, with a backhanded sweep, she smashes into a tree beside where Mama now stands, dumbfounded. Emma burbles in hysterics as Mama kneels down to her, finally maternal, but to the wrong person. I sashay towards them through the carnage. Even though I can't see myself, their swollen eyes tell me all I need to know.

I smile. I look great.

"Sissy, Jesse, please," Emma screams and grabs Mama like a shield. "I'm so sorry," she says. "I'm so, so sorry."

But I've been pretty clear on the value of words.

CLARA WALKER'S LITTLE DEATH

IT WAS JUST A LITTLE DEATH they'd asked for, but Clara Walker felt it tremble through the downshifted thrum of the night bugs and the tattered, tooth-yellow moonlight making décollage halos of the black water ripples around her bare thighs. A little death that had followed her down the hospital's porcelain-white hallways, past Charles and her mother poisoning each other with whispers in the waiting room, out to her truck and into the night. It rode with Clara until she stopped on an unmarked stretch of highway and let the distant surf of passing cars carry her into the tree line, into the swamp.

It followed her into the water, where Clara's every breath and movement troubled her dark reflection. One tremble, and her face wrinkled like her grandmother's had when she'd gone to join Grandpa. In a slower swell, however, Clara's rounded image was youthful in a way that she herself had never been, a child part her and part of the swamp. Clara's fingers danced like water spiders, attempting to recreate those momentary intersections of waves and vision.

Over the small splashes and the fly-buzz absence of the little death, she barely heard the movement on the bank behind her, but then a branch cracked and Clara turned. A light flickered and was quickly concealed. No animal, then, but the abortive shamble of poorly hidden footsteps along the dark, sucking shore.

"Hello?" Clara's empty, folded jeans on the bank were sudden leagues away.

In slow pieces, the woman's shape assembled itself from the pyramidal cypress shadows and scrimmage of thorns. She could have been Clara's mother's age, maybe, but shorter, softer. Curled like a fiddlehead, she gently lay something long and thin upon the ground before emerging in the moon's stark exposure.

"I know you." The woman tugged blanched, naked fingers.

Clara sank to her hips, the swamp soaking her shirt hem and wicking dark paths across her stomach.

"I don't think so," she replied.

"Sure," the woman said. "From the hospital."

Clara couldn't place her, but she'd been absorbed the whole time, neck-deep in the little death. This woman could have been anyone.

"Come with me," the woman said. She picked up a long, heavy-bladed machete from the ground. "Don't cause any trouble."

Clara obeyed and approached the shore.

Before Clara could reach her clothes, the woman grasped her arm, dragging her dripping from the water and then corralling her down the rumor of a deer path. When the path disappeared, the woman hacked through the overgrown plants, hewing forward, even though the sticks and stones of the emergent gateway pricked Clara and scratched staves across her blank thighs. Clara followed through the expanding ruin, finally emerging into a small copse of trees.

Once, this space might have counted as a clearing. The mare's nest of rough stones at the center might have enshrined the now-drowned fire pit. By shredded illumination sluicing through Spanish moss and miserly branches, Clara divined the serpentine rise and swell of funereal mounds and furrows. Unseen insects screamed murder from damp vegetable galleries, the unctuous miasma of interwoven blossoms and decay making the hot, wet air too much like drowning for Clara not to gasp.

The woman hooked the blade to a clasp on her belt. She picked up a shovel from the ground and planted its blade deep into the soil, standing the shaft like a naked signpost.

"Did you want to do it?" The woman walked toward Clara, the flashlight casting long shadows across the crevasses. "Was it your idea?"

CLARA WALKER'S LITTLE DEATH

"I don't . . . " Clara's heels caught a swell in the ground and she twisted, falling to her knees.

"Was it your idea?" the woman asked, suddenly appearing beside her. "Did you want to do it?"

"They did." Clara withdrew into her shoulders.

"You, though," the woman said, the blanket of her hot breath falling upon Clara's cheek. "Did you want it?"

Clara shook her head, then nodded, shrugged.

"Say it."

The woman curled down to hear the whispered croak of Clara's words. Beyond the flashlight's halo, the groans of frogs and crickets drowned Clara's confession, rendering it ripples in the night, but the woman nodded, satisfied. She stepped back, allowing the flashlight's corona to settle around them both.

In that moment of calm, the words released and flickering like fireflies, Clara embraced a new lightness. She laughed manic laughter. Unburdened, unfurling, she rose. She stretched wide, wider.

Clara grunted as the unexpected burden of the shovel's rough wood and heavy blade slapped across her palm. She opened her mouth, but the dull gleam of the machete on the woman's hip staunched any protest.

"That was the easy part," the woman said, swinging the machete's tip like a compass point, inscribing the gibbous arc back to the hollow impression of Clara's prostration. "Start digging."

"But I didn't . . . " Clara started, but the woman held up one thick finger to silence her.

"Dig until I tell you to stop."

Clara dug, each shovelful of slop building an ill pile. Her palms blistered and then ruptured, her back screamed, and she threw up. The hungry clay sucked at the shovel, pulling her deeper with each stroke.

"Do you always do what you're told?" the woman asked, perched on a lichen-shrouded stone and watching over Clara.

"What?" Clara stopped, blinking at the void that had grown up around her.

"Did I tell you to stop?"

Clara pulled the next shovelful up and let it fall on the soft, collapsing pile. The percussion of blood in her ears was deafening.

"Stop." The woman approached and held out her hand to take the shovel. "Now, lay down and bury yourself."

From the malformed trench, Clara's heart howled. "You don't have to do this," she said, and began to cry. "I could leave, just go home and pretend, you know."

"What will happen if I let you just leave?" The woman smiled, incongruously maternal for a moment, but then she crushed it. "Bury yourself."

"What if I say no?" Clara's eyes were wild, tears streaking the grime across her cheeks. Her thighs trembled, but the thick mud that held her feet smothered any flight.

"I'd like to see that." The woman held up the blade. "Really."

Clara surrendered and withered, shrinking into the hole.

After she pulled the last handful of muck on top of herself, Clara wriggled that last limb down into darkness, too. Above her, somewhere, the woman must have been waiting, but the sopping weight pressed into Clara's every pore, every orifice. Sealed in the wet mold of her body, she felt more than heard the ragged rasps of her own breath, a cold black mask filling her eyes and her ears.

Clara waited for the woman to tell her it was over, to give her permission to rise. It had to come soon, Clara thought as the soil squeezed her in its palm, or else she might never hear it.

All around her the earth was silent and black, commanding her to be still. Finally, the little death was silent, displaced by the large one on all sides. But inside Clara, something planted deeper than a root, deeper than a seed, twitched. It spoke.

"No."

Clara screamed, the sudden burst emptying her in a single giant bubble that erupted through the mud. Then she began to claw frantically upwards, reaching for the true stars. She felt the life inside her growing.

WE EAT DIRT AND SLEEP AND WAIT

OUTSIDE, THE WORMS ARE SINGING. The little ones are piping like songbirds in the black dirt packed against the buried house's windows. Others—much larger—cry like whales in the distance, and their calls reverberate through the earth until even the distant ridge of snow-capped mountains trembles like a jaw. Here in the house, deep in the soil, the timbers groan beneath the wormsong as the boy and the old woman wait.

In his bed, nestled in the folds of peeling ears of mushrooms, the blind boy trembles. He presses deeper into the pillows of mold sprouting in the living room's corner, as if trying to push himself into the safety of the floor.

The old woman enters from the kitchen, illuminated by the dim green glow of a lemonade pitcher that she's packed with luminescent soil. The boy falls still as he listens to the old woman pick her way around the furniture's quivering shadows and to his side. She rests a stained hand against his soft pink skin.

"Oh, my sweet one," she whispers. "You mustn't cry when the worms are just outside. We don't want them to find us, do we?"

The boy's white eyes roll towards her voice and his callused hands, pads worn down and devoid of nails, squirm around her wrist. His fingers crawl up her arm and towards her face, but she pulls away just before he reaches the wrinkles and creases that cut back from the corners of her parched lips. She places the lantern-pitcher on the table and sits in the chair beside him.

"My sweet one," she says again. "Let me tell you a story to keep you calm. It's one of your favorites."

There was an old woman who lived in a house with her husband. Their cozy home crowned a cul-de-sac of fine, sturdy structures nestled among emerald lawns. Although the two of them lived alone, the neighboring houses were filled to the walls with children and parents and pets all busy with their own lives. They had the common decency, however, to smile and wave as they passed by the old couple.

Every day, like a little clockwork, the old man would run his push mower across the lawn. Blades over blades, trimming down the tips and then raking them up. He did it in the spring when pink blooming brains of dogwood moped along the corners of the yard. He did it in the summer, when the smell of neighbors' charcoal lit the evenings. He did it in the fall, chewing over fire-colored leaves, and in the winter, too, churning the snow.

Every day, like a little cuckoo in her window, the old woman read her storybooks and watched her husband walking back and forth, back and forth. It was their little routine, and their lawn was their point of pride.

Then one day the husband's heart spring snapped. By the time the ambulance arrived, he was a delicate shade of robin's-egg blue.

Then the old woman still lived in a house, but she lived alone. After the funeral and the first few days of "we're sorry" casseroles, no one came to her porch or knocked on her door. Inside the empty house, she slept on just one side of a too-big bed. Groaning timbers followed her small steps up and down the stairs.

Outside, the grass still grew.

Taller and stronger, it grew darker and heavier from the deep black soil. With no one to trim it, the blades grew thick and high, until they reached the bottom of her window. Higher still it grew, until only her tiny silver head rose above the stalks like a dandelion's blowball. In one stiff breeze, it seemed, she might blow away.

The neighbors to her left told their teenage son to ask her if she needed help, but he didn't. The neighbors to their right said they would check on her, but never quite settled on when. Like a string of paste pearls melting one by one, their pretense at concern fell away and the neglect slid around the neighborhood, yet the old woman's lawn kept growing.

Eventually it covered the house.

The wind tented great fescues like praying hands over the roof. The fleshy tendrils of extraordinary bluegrass pressed against her windows and doors until it was as if the house was a face whose mouth and eyelids were being pinched closed.

The neighbors merely stared from their windows. If the old woman needed help, surely, all of them said, she would have asked. Since she hadn't, they told each other, she must enjoy being alone. It was easier for everyone this way.

And then the house sank into the lawn.

And as it sank, pulled down deeper by its weight and the deep roots of the grass, the old woman lay on her floor with her head in the fireplace. Through the creosote-choked flue she watched her one pinch of blue sky shrink until it was finally eclipsed. The tears she cried traced pale paths across her soot-stained cheeks until they, too, were buried.

And above the house, the hole closed up and the grass grew back. Only the empty lawn was left where the house had stood.

That problem solved itself, the neighbors said, but it was never quite true. Every summer since then, when the nights are heavy as deep black soil, all the lawns in the neighborhood sing like cuckoos. Each blade of grass weeps every time it's trimmed.

Now, the old woman still lives in the house, deeply buried. She has adapted, though, as best she can. For drinking, a taproot pierces the ceiling and drips into her mouth. Outside her window are minerals rich enough to eat, one muddy handful at a time. At night she reads her storybooks by the soil-light and dreams of burning dragon bones for coal. She dreams of witches and elves and sweet little children.

Without her stories, she would have gone quite mad.

Until one day there was a knock at the door.

GORDON B. WHITE

In the thick night outside the walls, the wormcalls still echo. The cries roll through empty pockets and reflect from stained quartz obelisks, seeming to come from every side: Where the front yard had been, but which is now black soil, the worms are singing. From the garden patch that is now black soil, the worms are singing. From the blue squint of sky above the chimney that the leaves of grass choked off and which is now black soil, the worms are singing.

In the underground house, the boy stirs in his fungal bed and whimpers again. The old woman opens the window and scoops a handful of dirt from the wall of earth outside. Palm caked, she presses it to the boy's mouth, but he turns away from the offer. The boy moans again, as if calling out to the darkness, but the woman shushes him.

"Oh, my sweet one," the old woman says. "You need not fear. We are together." She trembles, though, as her tongue flicks out, testing the air. "I'll tell you another if you will just keep calm."

There was a lonely young boy—almost a baby, truly—who lived in a house deep in the woods. His father drove a tow truck and his mother did nothing but her nails, so all day he was left to his own devices, playing in the mud of the yard. He pulled back flat rocks and wondered at the pillbugs beneath. He dug with sticks and stones, humming to himself as he did. In the evening, his mother attacked his hands with bristle brushes and his little fingers squirmed, chafed pink from the scrubbing.

On some nights, however, when the moon was full and the clouds were thin, they all packed up the truck and headed down to the sump. On those nights his parents' blood was high, and the conditions were best for "Squirm-hooking."

Were there once other, more reverent names for the Squirms? Surely, but the few invocations to the Father-Mothers of the fragrant soft darkness remained as skip rope rhymes or half-joking prayers for fertility in the field or the bed. The Squirms the boy's parents knew were paltry things—almost babies, truly—no bigger than an arm, little like the leviathan annelids that once ground boulders to loam through their gizzard and crop. The boy's parents took great pleasure in tormenting those degenerate things.

The squirm-hooking site wasn't far from the road, but to the little boy being next to the pit was like waiting to be swallowed by a whole other world. The sump's lips were soft, but his father would back the tow truck right up to the edge. The taillights smeared the pit of sludge below, painting it red where the ground was weak and wet and strange things crawled. On those wild nights, the muck shook with their singing. It was no place for a child, clearly, so the boy was left in the truck to press his face to the glass.

Down came the truck's boom, and the boy's father would spool out the hook and the cable with enough slack from the winch to reach a good depth. Then they dressed the hook with whatever road-killed carcass was handy and stuffed it with rocks. They chucked it over the edge.

Down the hook sank with its ponderous bait. Down through the loose soil where the baby Squirms played. The boy's parents waited.

Then a little one would strike.

The line would go taut and the boy's mother would shriek and his father would laugh and the winch would groan in protest. With the cable suckered by the Squirm's front-skin, the creature would writhe like a single great muscle. Once fully extracted from the earth, it grunted and squealed as it flailed in the air.

The boy's mother and father were only casual brutes, and there was neither method nor art in the way they would fall on the Squirms. A tire iron. A crowbar. Work boots. A rock. They pounded until its skin peeled back and the pulp of its ruin spoiled the air. Crying, the boy would beat his fists on the back window, but it only drove them into further frenzy.

Afterwards, they would ride back to the house, the car sweet with sweat and the rotten smell of Squirm innards. Many nights the boy was thankful to be sent to bed without supper.

Then, one night, a big one struck.

It hit the bait with a great yank, and the line sang out and the sump's earthen lip gave way. The tow truck tilted and sank into the ground. The last thing the boy saw was his parents gasping and blinking in the headlights as he was pulled below. Was the look on their face one of horror? Of joy?

Then the boy was gone, a passenger in a truck pulled through the darkness in the giant Squirm's tow. Every push and contraction took him further, further, further down.

Then the line broke and the great worm pressed on, and the boy was left in silence. With the back window cracked, he pushed into the moist hold of aerated soil. There was barely enough space to breathe; there was just barely enough for the boy to push forward a little more.

He cried at first, but then the worms cried back. Then they circled back and then circled around. In a few more passes, the crying turned to singing, and in a few more after that, they all sang the same song. So the little boy followed them.

Was it days, months, or even years that the boy crawled in the mushy wake of the great Mother-Fathers as they pistoned through their mucus-slick tunnels? The boy pawed at the dirt until his nails peeled back from their beds and his fingertips wore down smoother than clay. Pressing face forward, he wriggled on until his eyes were stained soil-green, then were bleached, and then gone.

Over time, he inched through the Fields of Calcite Stars like a naked and slow-flying comet. At the Forest of Deep Roots, he picked his way through the clearings left by the gargantuan worms. He drew moisture and nutrients from the humus of the Great Squirms' rich feces. What adventures the little boy had in the Great Squirms' trail!

Until one day, the plates beneath the earth all shifted and the boy and the Squirms were pulled apart. No matter how much he sang and then cried and pressed on alone in the darkness, he found nothing until he came across the underground house. Even though he could not see it, he felt the walls and the eaves resisting his vibrations as he crawled.

He knocked on the door.

———— ∿∿ ————

"Then the old woman let the boy in," the old woman says. "She let him sleep there. She fed him. She told him stories at night. He owed her so much and so wanted to stay with her that when she told him to be quiet, he was a good little boy. Do you understand?"

In the deep house, however, the story has not calmed the boy. He still writhes beneath the pummeling songs of the great creatures beyond the walls. In a spasm, he calls out and makes as if to rise, but the old woman pushes down his forehead. She slides her other hand across his mouth, stifling his cries.

"Quiet," she says. "Must I tie you down?"

The boy thrashes, but the woman presses down on him until he is almost smothered and her dirt-stained tongue clucks above his blank eyes. The air is cloyingly sweet.

"What if I tell you one more story?" she asks. "It's one you've never heard, but should keep you still."

The blind boy whimpers once more, but then is quiet. Down here, with windows of black soil and night's dirt packed around the walls, there are no sights to see. The only things they have are stories, and time.

The old woman licks her lips and begins.

———— ✺ ————

There was another old woman who lived in a house next to a sweet little boy and a wicked young girl. The little girl gossiped and spun lies like a silkworm. She called the old woman a witch, which wasn't quite true. Not yet.

Like all old women, she had been young once upon a time. She had once had a husband and a son, although tragedy took the latter and the former left soon after. So she moved into the little house, where she told herself stories about how sweet it would be to have her little boy back. He would be happy to see her, of course, and she would be so pleased that she could just eat him up. Once reunited, no more would they part.

Despite her best intentions, it must be admitted that all those years alone had made the old woman loose in her manners. Hungry for company, she would stare from her windows at the passing children, waiting for them to stray onto her lawn. As soon as a little foot touched the first of the grass blades, she would burst out like a trapdoor spider, framed by the tendrils of her frayed yellowed hair.

That was the game the children played, and they called it "Dance on Your Grave." They would try to draw the witch out and then run away. Laughing and screaming, it was all great fun.

Then she caught one.

It was a very early spring day, just on the tail-tip of winter, when the old woman caught the young girl's brother. Her fingernails were pitted like rotten teeth in wrinkled gums, and when they sank into the brother's jacket, they bit through and held on. No matter how much the children screamed, the old woman held on.

"Come with me," the old woman shrieked as she pulled. "I'm sorry, I'm sorry. Let me show you I've changed."

Was she confused? Was she telling the truth? The wicked little girl did not pause to ask, but instead lashed out to defend her brother. Her wild fist caught the side of the old woman's mouth. The soft old skin tore.

Everyone froze. The tatter of flesh flapped for a moment; then the old woman quietly pressed it back to her face. Dancing like a millipede, she skittered back across the lawn.

After that, the wicked little girl told more stories. That the old woman dug holes like a wrinkly beetle, tunneling under her yard so that she could spring up from below. That she wore a mask and tasted children's fear and loved it. Most of these were lies, of course.

The girl told her parents, too, but they didn't want to believe her. A problem neighbor is a problem, but a problem child is worse. She was lucky, they said, that the police hadn't been called.

For a week, the girl was grounded, and she sat by her window. Despite her vigil, nothing seemed to move at the old woman's house. The windows were empty and dark beneath the flat grey sky.

Then one night, without warning, it snowed.

It was a very late snow, and the sound of the soft wet flakes slapping against the window stirred the girl from her slumber. It was so cold that the wooden floor prickled her feet and the house's ribs groaned like a ship. Below her, cold cruel things swam in the depths.

WE EAT DIRT AND SLEEP AND WAIT

Was it a sound, perhaps, that drew her from her room? A displaced pressure in the air that pulled her down the hall? Did she follow clouds of steam that rose from the floorboards' cracks as if the ground below was exhaling? Like a ghost, did those breaths slide beneath her brother's door?

When she finally opened the door, her brother's bed was empty. The impression of his body still clung to the white sheets. She screamed so loud that she shook the ground.

The policemen came, but found nothing. All the doors were still locked, and the snow outside his window was undisturbed.

Two days later, when the snow all melted, the signs of its passing were evident. The saturated mud sucked at each footstep. Branches lay cast down and broken. Bent stick arms held a carrot nose and two wet coal eyes where a snowman had been.

And reaching out like a crooked finger from the old woman's window towards the little girl's house was a single deep depression, as if an insect's tunnel had collapsed beneath the lawn.

The girl's parents gathered the neighbors and they rang the old woman's doorbell. They banged on the windows. They broke down the door. They went into her basement and in it found neither bricks nor concrete, only a pit of raw dark soil and a now filled-in hole. It was possible, the detectives later said, that she'd been inside when the weight of the late winter snow had weakened the ground above. When it thawed, of course, she would have been stuck.

The policemen came again and dug up the yard, but found neither bodies nor bones. There was nothing below. The little girl's brother was never found.

But the old woman still lived, though not in her house. Trapped in the sopping tunnel, she dug further until she lost her way. Her full belly dragged as her wicked nails carved deeper and deeper, but she grew leaner and leaner the deeper she dug. The torn flesh of her face pulled away further as the rocks tugged at the muscles and chipped her teeth away. Her yellow eyes turned black with the grit, then red, and then she cried thick, dark tears.

She might have wandered forever, but she came across the house buried in the dirt. Her fingers scrabbled on the rooftop's slate, so up to the apex she squirmed. She squeezed herself into the chimney. Finally, she emerged from the fireplace, blacker than night.

Pressed beside the hearth, she watched as another old woman shuffled into the living room with a pitcher of glowing green soil half-lighting her way. A little pink boy squirmed in the corner. The doddering old woman, unaware of the hidden one, sat down on her couch and began to tell the boy stories.

As the hidden woman crouched in the corner, she listened to the stories, and then she heard it. She knew! The boy in the stories, the one in the house, the one here beneath the ground—he must be hers! Now, she knew, they could make a home again. They could be together. Forever.

She was so happy to be reunited that she could just eat him up. But not yet, not like this.

The hidden woman rose slowly. As she unfolded herself, the last tatters of her flesh fell away. Raw and naked, she crept into the kitchen. She dug her nails into the walls' peeling plaster and drew herself high into the corner like a spider. She licked her crooked teeth and waited.

Later, as the boy slept, the storyteller rose from his side. The hidden woman counted the unsteady footsteps and watched the spill of the pitcher's trembling light approach the kitchen. She held her breath and waited.

She dropped like a shadow from the ceiling.

Later, for a while, she was full again, and happy. She dressed herself anew in old skins and, except for the rips by the eyes and mouth, the face she wore didn't even look like a mask.

She kept feeding the boy, though, letting him sleep and grow heavy. One way or another, they would be together forever.

Until, one night, the worms began to sing.

———— ∾ ————

Outside, the worms are singing. The little ones are chirping like alarms. Like mother whales, eyeless, the giant ones call out to their lost calf. They cut through the soil's abyssal pressure in the exercise of something deeper than instinct. Their songs echo from every corner as if they are drawing the knot of all their tunnels tighter towards the house at the center.

The boy will not stop crying, and so the old woman sighs, and from within the folds of her dress she pulls a kitchen knife. She draws the blade across her mouth, cheek to cheek, and peels back the skin of her lips. Her chipped and crooked teeth glow green in the soil-light and set every shape and shadow trembling.

"I'll never let you go again," she whispers. "I love you so."

She rests a hand against his soft pink skin, pulling his head back to expose his throat. Instead of falling silent, though, the boy wails and the piercing tone from his quivering lips melds with the tremors from beyond the walls into a twisting harmony. For a moment, their music intertwines and the whole house hums. The old woman fumbles her hand to cover his mouth and smother his song, but it is too late.

The house's front wall shudders beneath a heavy blow.

The door bursts open.

THE SPUTTERING WICK
OF THE STARS

IT IS THE PEOPLE IN the small towns dotting the countryside who first notice the darkness in the evening skies. One by one, the stars are vanishing. Every night, more are snuffed out: hundreds, thousands, hundreds of thousands of light years away. The encroaching blackness rolls across the horizon like a glacial wave.

As the patch of empty sky grows, eating away the constellations, the world cannot cope. First comes violence, then self-harm; local panic, then global paralysis. One by one the power grids go out, the communication lines fall silent. The darkness spreads across the earth, reflected in the pooling abyss above.

Here in Asheford, in the now-black village center, the remaining congregants gather in the chapel each night, waiting. From sunset to sunrise, the Reverend Mott hovers around the lectern, illuminated by a single large white candle. He rails against the sinners that have brought this plague of shadow, harrowing the sunken-eyed living and the long-since dead.

"Hell is real." The reverend wrings his hands, casting claws of shadow across his flock as he paces between the candle and the silent mass. "This darkness is the void, the absence of the light of the Lord."

He stops and crooks his finger at the room. "The Beast is coming for us. A cold, black wind from out of space. The very breath of the Devil is blowing out the stars like candles."

The flame flickers, and a woman in the pews begins to weep.

But there is a different murmuring in the back of the nave. A man stands, pushing someone away, then strides up the aisle towards Reverend Mott.

"I'm sorry, but I can't let you go on." The man reaches the steps and climbs to Mott's level. "This is all superstition. It's lies."

Reverend Mott crosses his arms and roots himself between the man and the fire. "What do you know? Hubris like yours has brought this ill wind."

"First of all," the man adjusts his glasses, "there's no wind in space, ill or otherwise. There's no air at all. The stars are not being blown out."

"What, then, is causing the darkness? What is this, if not evil's breath and the world's end?"

"Let me tell you." The man turns to the crowd. "I am a scientist. I know the truth." He rolls up his sleeves, gesticulating as he speaks. "You see, I've studied the universe. I've seen it through telescopes in all its wonder and strangeness. I promise you, there is no magic wind; the Devil is not blowing out stars through the reaches of space."

The man swings his hands in punctuation, forcing Mott to take a half step backwards to keep his balance. The crowd mutters.

"No, instead what it's doing"—the man licks his thumb and index finger—"is more like this."

He reaches past the Reverend Mott and pinches the candle's wick, snuffing the flame instantly and unleashing darkness throughout the chapel.

"But you were right. The Beast is coming."

ULTRAMARINE

CHERYL RODE IN THE PASSENGER seat, eyes closed, listening to the radio and pretending to sleep. When Derek began to turn down the volume and cleared his throat, she stirred. "Leave it," she murmured. "No more talking."

He guided them off the highway at a no-name exit, down dark roads without signs. Cheryl felt the tires bump as the paved roads became gravel and dirt. She only opened her eyes when Derek killed the engine and she heard the headlights click off.

For a moment, the darkness beyond the windows seemed to swallow them. Yet as her eyes adjusted, the radiance of the moon and stars outside swelled in intensity. The world beyond them wasn't black, but rather the same deep cerulean as photographs of the ocean.

"Why are we stopped?" Cheryl asked, frowning. They were on the edge of an embankment, the ground dropping away beyond the hood. "Where are we?"

Derek opened his door and climbed out.

"Come on," he said, squinting into the distance. "You've got to see this."

"What is it now?" Cheryl asked, craning her neck, but unable to see more than darkness. She slowly unbuckled her seatbelt, sighing as she opened the door and dragged herself out into the warm, heavy air.

"Come on," Cheryl said. "What can—oh, wow."

Below them stretched a boundless pool of black water tinged with electric blue. The stars above shone back from the still center of the lake, but azure sparks burst and receded within the waves lapping at the shoreline. Their movement spawned brighter, closer cosmos.

"Is that—is it a reflection? What is it?"

"Bioluminescence," Derek said. "Tiny microorganisms." He scrabbled down the embankment and Cheryl followed, pulled towards the border of this strange new universe.

Fixed between the glow of the lake and the gleam of the stars, the world around them looked pale and frozen. Cheryl wrapped her arms around Derek from behind as he stared out towards the shimmering horizon.

"It's gorgeous," she said.

"One of the university guys told me about it," he said. "They come out here to watch for meteors, and it isn't normally like this, but recently—well." He shrugged and gestured beyond them.

"Is it dangerous?" she asked.

"No," he said, twisting within her grip, just enough to turn around and pull her close. "It's a natural phenomenon."

———

Cheryl hadn't been skinny-dipping in years and Derek had never been, but here, in the strange countryside with the warm night and the cool electric illumination, they felt like different people on a different planet.

Like miniature novas, billows of ozone blue swirled and faded around their feet as they waded in. It churned around their legs, their torsos, their arms. When the water reached her waist, Cheryl dove in. She cut a trail of fire through the water before breaking the surface, dripping with luminosity. Her body was electric and starlight rivulets traced over her skin.

Derek followed suit, far less graceful but no less dramatic when he burst from the shimmering water. Sparks flew from his fingertips before quickly fading back into darkness.

Their every movement stirred up haloes. Flashing coronas silhouetted them against the black water and the moonlight.

"Do you like it?" he asked.

"I love it," she said.

They were silent for a while.

"What makes it glow?" she asked. "Why does it do this?"

"I'm not sure," Derek said, sinking down to his chin and paddling over to her. "It doesn't, usually."

Cheryl sensed another lecture, but as Derek's hands moved against her legs and the small of her back, she didn't mind. She could float here until the end of the world.

She gave over to the water and the stars.

To Derek.

"Some things use bioluminescence as camouflage," Derek began. "Because from underneath"—he cupped his hands and threw the water into the air, where the droplets sparkled and, for a moment, seemed to join the stars—"it looks like the night sky."

Cheryl crouched down, dipping her head beneath the surface. It seemed that she could see bursts of light even through her eyelids, and the pulse in her ears was an encompassing thrum, as if everything around her was enormously alive.

She emerged. The glowing liquid framed the corners of her smile. "What else?" she said.

"Well," Derek said, brushing slowly past her. "Some creatures use it to attract a mate."

In the dark water between them, he traced the shape of a Valentine heart with his finger. Although the edges faded almost as quickly as he drew them, as he repeated the gesture again and again, the afterimage seemed to linger.

He stopped. The now-dark water swirled. His smile and her eyes shone in the moonlight.

"And some creatures use it," Derek said, still smiling as he sank into the water until it reached his chin, "to catch their prey!" He leapt towards her with a mock growl. Cheryl squealed and pushed him away as he made gnashing sounds and pretended to eat her face.

He let go and slid back into the water. Cheryl giggled, catching her breath.

"You bastard," she said as she swung her open hand across the top of the dark water. A luminous spray skimmed from the surface, hitting Derek in the eyes. "I love—"

Derek, laughing, wiped at his face. "You love what?" he said, rubbing his eyes for a moment before opening them.

But he was alone.

"Cheryl?" he said. "Cheryl?"

He watched the still dark waters, looking for ripples, waiting for Cheryl to emerge.

But there was nothing.

He looked towards the shore, expecting, now praying, to see her emerge from the shallows and walk in glowing footsteps onto the land.

But the shoreline was empty.

And while Derek was looking towards the shore, he missed the frantic bursts of submarine electricity erupting and dissipating behind him.

Sinking deeper and deeper, they pulsed like dying stars being pulled into the black hole at the center of the lake.

THE LURE OF THE LOLLIPOP TREE

JIM KNOWS HE'S DONE A bad thing, but still he bursts into the bedroom, positively glowing, and before Laurie can finish asking where he's been, he's talking over her, burying her beneath words and gestures. It's imperative, he feels, to get this out.

"I was out walking," he says. "Longer than usual, yes, but it's only—oh. I had no idea. See, I was over past the park on this street I'd never been on before and, Laurie, there was this house and, oh, it was perfect."

Jim settles down on the edge of the bed, crushing the mattress and pinning Laurie beneath the blankets. Despite the outside world's recent brief stab at springtime, a chill has returned.

"Not that this place," he barely breathes, "I mean, our place, isn't also wonderful, but that house was a real *house* house, you know? It was like the ones you draw as a kid when you're supposed to make a picture of your family. Square body, two stories, a triangle roof, even a little tree outside with its leaves trimmed in a perfect circle like a lollipop." He sighs in an extended deflation.

He finally looks at Laurie. "Your eyes are red."

She rubs at her lashes. "Just allergies."

"The weather, sure," Jim says. "But this house, Laurie. And inside it was just so cozy."

"You went inside?"

Jim's face burns in response.

"No, no, no." Laurie fights out from beneath the sweltering covers. "Not again."

"It's not like that." Jim reaches out, but she shrinks towards the bed's far side. "I won't—I can't—keep apologizing."

Despite her retreat, a desire has unfurled within him. He had practically run home, eager to do more than talk and, since Laurie cannot withdraw any further without falling, Jim slides across. He picks up her hand and kisses it.

"I'm sorry," he says. "For everything. I love you."

"I'm exhausted." Laurie pushes against Jim's chest, but he doesn't move.

"Please?" Jim whimpers, the burn inside him curling over on itself, trying a different tactic as he plants his head against Laurie's chest. Above him she sniffles, and Jim can hear an emptiness that rattles beneath her skin. He wants to fill it.

"I mean, you're happy here, but . . . " He trails off. "Don't you still love me?"

She pauses, but not long enough to cool him down.

"Okay," Laurie says. She lies back and closes her tired eyes.

After they finish and Laurie rolls her back to him for the night, Jim wanders the strange house they keep. His footsteps and fingertips leave faint glittered traces across the naked floors and bare eggshell walls. Even with only the sparse furniture they'd hauled across the country, this place is too constricting. Life here is only a television room, a kitchen, a bedroom, a bathroom and a half, and the spare room that Laurie insisted they make into an office. Where is there to grow or run wild?

In the morning, Laurie will rise and fold herself into her starched attire that it feels like Jim only ever sees from behind. She'll drive to her new office in this new city, her absence a tangible presence for twelve hours until she comes home and her presence becomes an absence—immediately pajama-clad, but still answering work emails. Since he's still jobless, by day Jim will clean, cook, and keep the house that Laurie wants. He will bear the chafe of domestication as penance for what he did and why Laurie had insisted they either uproot together or split apart. He had agreed to the move because that dissolution would have been one failure too many.

THE LURE OF THE LOLLIPOP TREE

Yet as Jim stares at their sterile décor, he can't help but think about that other house. What he didn't tell Laurie was that the perfect house wasn't just one that a child might draw, but the one that he *had* drawn. That crayon lines came to life before him and it wasn't just the perfect representation of a house, but the house where he had always known that he would grow a family. His parents, his teachers, his instincts had told him so. This desire has been secretly growing in the cracks between what Jim wants and what he has, but after seeing that perfect house tonight, his nesting instinct is in full bloom. It makes these walls Laurie has pressed him between squeeze even tighter.

He also hadn't told her, even though she'd known, but he'd gone inside. Unlike Laurie's house, the perfect house had been as warm and still as a breath held between clasped hands. It was like a pitcher that his recollections filled until he was sinking in them. The carpet's deep fingers held the not unpleasant must of solid wood furniture. In the living room he had glimpsed the heavy coffee table and pilled couch reposed before the boxy cathode ray television. He didn't even need to look to know that above the fireplace hung that final family portrait of five-year-old Jim sandwiched between both parents, smiling for posterity. The landing was just as he imagined remembering it, down to the side table's blue vase pinching pink orchids and the violet runner up the stairs to the second floor.

How could he convey to Laurie that poetry of space that even now is breaking apart and re-setting his bones? How he feels the traditional masculine drive to procreate and to provide growing like a tree inside him? If he even tried to tell Laurie, she would think he was blaming her again.

Moreover, Jim could never tell her about the shape he'd seen in the upstairs bedroom window. He could never tell Laurie what he had done inside and what he'd brought back.

～

Laurie's dry heaves interrupt Jim's dreams of backyards swallowed by kudzu. Shower steam curls into the hall as Jim approaches the wedge of light spilling from the bathroom. Her retching grows softer, wearier, as he opens the door.

Laurie, pitched over the toilet, clutches a beige towel like a cocoon she isn't ready to shed, even as her wet flesh tries to convulse free. Another tremor rises, but she swallows it, eyes pink from the strain.

"Are you sick?" Jim asks.

"Food poisoning." Uneasy steps take her to the sink and the fogged-over mirror.

"I thought we ate the same things." It's too early, of course, but Jim still tries to divine any changes beneath her terry sheath. "Do you think you're—you know?"

Laurie's hand cuts through the condensation on the mirror, exposing Jim where he looms behind her like a rumpled ghost.

"No," Laurie says to their reflections.

Humidity kisses the mirror's silver back into fog, rendering husband and wife as dim portraits, then shadows, then nothing.

Jim watches Laurie closely because he knows her every day is a busy day, daisy-chaining into a busy week, a busy month, and a busy forever. Because he knows she can never be too sick for work, he watches as she rearranges things to be too sick for home and schedules around her lingering morning *discomfort*. Even as it drags into the second week she insists it's a bug, and turns in for bed so early that the lights are off before Jim embarks on his evening constitutionals.

Jim spends every evening failing to find the perfect house again. The world, briefly in bloom during that strawberry spring, has closed back up like a tight little blossom, but the wandering lets Jim's memory return again and again to his favorite room in the perfect house. It was a nursery with petal-yellow walls and an empty crib, guarded by a limp mobile of purple blossoms among fat and fuzzy bees. A mural of vines crept up from the baseboard, green fingers reaching like beanstalks towards the stick-on stars that glowed on the ceiling. Even though Jim had never seen a room like that, he felt like he had been raised there. Even now, it consumes his thoughts as the perfect place for offspring.

After Laurie's illness began, Jim had managed to leave her alone for two whole weeks, but after one particularly late jaunt during which the return of the frigid air's return has shaken his faith in the bargain he thought he'd made, he can no longer resist checking. That night, as Jim slips into bed beside Laurie, he clenches his hands into fists over and over. When circulation returns and they are warm, almost hot, Jim slides them up under Laurie's nightshirt. Pressing between her hips, just below her belly button, he tries to feel the seed growing. There—a little lump like a peach pit. Soon its roots will be so deep that Laurie can no longer pretend it isn't there. She'll have to slow down, maybe even quit her job, and Jim can reassume his place as breadwinner and reclaim the respect that he deserves. Things will be as they should: Jim will procreate and Jim will provide. The vision is already sprouting in his mind.

Jim is a film running at too many frames per second. Finally having found a purpose, he sheds the malingering and sulking that had defined his life in Laurie's house. Now, while Laurie is off-camera, the sun races the sky in fast-forward and Jim scurries like a carpenter ant from garage to home improvement store to spare room and back, as if following a pheromone trail. When Laurie returns, the film speed resets, and they eat dinner in an exhausted and almost comfortable silence. She goes to bed and, worn to contentment, Jim joins her without his nightly ramble. The next day, they repeat without complaint.

Then one day Jim shuts the door to the spare room, and he's glowing again. That night at dinner, he asks leading questions intended to goad Laurie into her former office.

"Do we have a stapler?" Jim asks. "Where do you suppose our tax documents are?" Finally, "When was the last time you used the office?"

But Laurie does not rise to take the bait. "I'm exhausted," she says. "You're home all day, can't you handle things on your own?"

Jim hunches over a pad of paper, working out the next problem beneath a flurry of pencil sketches. With the first step finished, Jim's hands and brain itch, and so the graphite streaks fall like rain as he layers up concept after concept. He's so absorbed by his ferocious drawing that he doesn't notice Laurie enter, and when she finally speaks, he jumps.

"What are you doing?" she asks.

He sprawls across the drawings like a boy hiding dirty pictures, but then a grin blooms. Jim spreads his arms to reveal two houses, unalike in form or composition.

On one page is the childishly simple reference drawing of his perfect house. Organically symmetrical in unwavering lines, the square body wears a pointed roof like a party hat. Four crosshatched windows at two per level stare out like insect eyes around the mouth of the door. A single lollipop tree rises as enticement from the empty yard. There is no depth or perspective; it's just this symbol that has wormed its way into Jim.

On the other page is their current single-story house, unmade and remade in half a dozen skeletal variations striving towards the ideal. Here, a dozen posts sprout like legs to raise it up another story— there, its top has exploded and new beams like fingers grasp towards the sky. The house is squashed, stretched, cut apart or aggregated with others, all of the hash marks striving to make the domestic one into the alien other.

At the bottom of the page stand two little figures. One is a stick-figure man, limbs as thin as a pen line. The other has the sharp triangle of a skirt indicating a woman, but her belly is as round as the lollipop tree.

"Ah," is all Laurie musters.

"It'll make sense when it's done," Jim says, and returns to scratching away.

Laurie's hand flutters like a leaf down to Jim's shoulder. "I need you to come to the doctor with me. Please."

Jim grunts, still drawing. "I'm fine."

"It's about me."

Jim puts his pencil down. He smiles. "Of course, darling. That's what responsible husbands do."

THE LURE OF THE LOLLIPOP TREE

Rising, Jim takes Laurie in his arms, and she plants her face in surrender against his shoulder. Her breathing permeates his shirt until his desires swell again like moss in a drizzle.

"Let me show you what else they can do," he whispers.

Jim steers Laurie down the hall to the spare room she still thinks is her office. With a flourish, he opens the door and reveals yellow walls, painted plants, a crib's empty cage, and pale press-on stars that glimmer from the ceiling.

"Oh, Jim," she whispers.

"I knew you'd love it." He beams and turns to search her face for his good work's reward.

"Oh, Jim," she whispers again, and closes her eyes, tight, against his hungry gaze.

The expanse of Laurie's belly glistens like the flesh of a rare tropical fruit as the technician runs an ultrasound wand over the gel. Gradually, the static on the screen coalesces, and all three of them—Laurie, Jim, the tech—try to interpret the signs.

Jim and Laurie haven't spoken since he unveiled the nursery. Last night she slept hanging off the bed, as if even an accidental touch could kill her. In the chill of the examination room, however, she clings to him as they wait for the tech to tell them what the ultrasound's pen-and-ink grain reveals.

"A fetus at this stage," the tech says, holding her fingers a pinch apart, "would be about yea big. Size of a bean, maybe." The tech points to the screen. "This isn't right."

Laurie squeezes Jim's knuckles hard enough to pop them. "What is it, then?"

The tech hems and haws. "I should get the doctor, if that's all right. We do that in"—she pauses—"special cases."

Laurie nods with the resignation of someone whose consent is a formality.

The tech glances once more at Laurie's chart. "And you haven't been on any medication other than . . . " She flips back. "Anxiety? And allergies?"

"It's been a rough year," Laurie says.

"Of course." The tech excuses herself from the room.

Jim creeps an arm around Laurie's shoulder, and she sinks beneath the pressure. He kisses her forehead and follows her line of sight out the window, to where thin branches hold a few bitter leaves that had been coaxed out by the intemperate mid-winter spring, then left to freeze.

"What's happening?" Laurie mutters.

Whispering hush-a-byes, Jim pulls her closer. He doesn't tell her, but on the ultrasound screen, in the smears and wash that Laurie and the tech couldn't decipher, Jim can see it staring right at them—four eyes like windows, lips pursed like a door, a crown like a peaky little roof. The light in the upstairs window even winks at him.

Jim never told Laurie that the golden glow behind the gauze curtain in the perfect house's upstairs window had drawn him in like a moth. He never told her how a swaying silhouette had danced out from the depths of the well lit, yet hidden, room. How it beckoned to him.

There was a perfume on the air that night, just a subtle hint of those early-blooming plants teased out by the unseasonable warmth. After a long winter, alone in Laurie's house, Jim hadn't been feeling himself. He'd been cooped up, confined until only these brief walking furloughs from his prison could keep him from lashing out. That pent-up energy was the only reason, really, that he'd entered. The only reason he'd behaved the way he did inside.

Honeyed light had oozed from the slit along the front door's jamb. It spread like eager lips beneath his bold push, and inside the house smelled like hardwood's spice and the leaves of yellowed books. At first slowly, as if sunk in resin but pressing onwards, Jim gave himself an abbreviated tour of the living room, the dining room, the kitchen. He paused for a great long while in the nursery, letting it fill him with the desire to fill it in turn.

He wasn't thinking clearly. The neurons in his head were sparkling like gold dust. They weren't Jim's feet that were drawn up the stairs, down the darkened hall and past closed doors, towards the illumination beyond. They weren't Jim's hands that opened the door to the well-lit room that had lured him inside.

As vivid as the rest of the house remains, the woman in the bedroom is hazy. Jim remembers how she had seemed to float before the window. How the lamp's glow had cast her skin in an almost lavender hue and drawn out a shadow that stretched to the ceiling. How her eyes seemed dark, her pursed lips rose-red, and how he tried to circle her naked body, but the misfiring hormonal overload of his scattered memories can only recall how she shivered like a paper doll, almost insubstantial from the wrong angle.

Jim didn't tell Laurie any of this because it wasn't him, really. The Jim who had hung his head and followed Laurie across the country would never have run his fingers over a stranger's petal-soft skin. He would never have peeled off his clothes and pulled that stranger down onto the lily-white expanse of the master bed. He would never have done that again. It had been a different Jim in that house.

But, oh, the things that Jim did within her soft folds.

***

Jim's cellphone flashes *LAURIE* as it beeps in the car's passenger seat and pulls his attention away from the streets that he's been cruising. He reaches over to answer and puts it on speaker. "Hey, sweetie," he says, eyes going back to the passing houses. "How's the business trip?"

There is a pregnant pause before she answers. "It wasn't business, Jim."

"What?" He looks over to where her voice sits beside him like a ghost, but finds only his reflection in the passenger's window. "You lied to me?"

"No, Jim. I told you everything," Laurie says, briefly heated but chilling quickly. "You just only ever hear what you want." A sigh rolls across the waves that bring her distant voice to him. "Anyway, it's done now and I'm okay."

Jim swallows the lump in his throat. "What's done?"

"The procedure. Fiona is here with me, and I'll be discharged tomorrow. I've already missed too much work. But I think . . . I think . . . " she echoes, and fades.

Suddenly her sister's voice breaks through. "You need to be gone, Jim. Laurie needs space after the way you ruined—"

There's a scuffle, and then Laurie is back. "Sorry. But yes. I need some time."

"Ruined?" Jim asks. "What about the baby?"

Another pause. "You know it wasn't a baby."

His lips curl towards screaming, but Jim steadies himself. "The fetus, then," he says.

"It wasn't a fetus."

Realization stakes Jim through the gut.

"Was it"—he drops his voice to a whisper, barely containing the nervous energy. "It was a seed, wasn't it?"

"It was a tumor, Jim."

The static of a bad connection ebbs like a black tide between them.

"Jim?" Laurie's voice is gentle, if not calm. "These thoughts you've been having, they aren't real. You know that, right?"

"What do you mean?" He realizes that he hasn't been paying proper attention. He might have missed the house.

"The spare room. The procedure. Us."

"You can't blame me for wanting a family, Laurie."

"I don't," she says. "But right now—"

"Your career. I know."

"There's more to it."

"I can't keep apologizing," Jim snaps. "Maybe if you had . . . or I hadn't . . . if we . . . " He pulls over and puts the car into park. "I'm sorry," he stabs his finger at the empty seat, "but I moved all the way across the country for that. For you. Why isn't that enough?"

"It's not about being enough," Laurie says. "Won't you please let me help you?"

Jim laughs. "It isn't supposed to be like that."

"It's okay. Really. I can keep—"

"I don't need help, Laurie!"

The line is quiet.

THE LURE OF THE LOLLIPOP TREE

"Okay," she says.

"Okay," he says. For half a minute they just breathe at one another, until Jim clears his throat.

"The"—he can't call it what she thinks it is—"the thing from inside you. Bring it home, please? I want to see it."

———

Jim had thrown himself into that strange woman in the perfect house that night. Everything he'd done to spoil Laurie's trust, back before she found out and made them move, he did it again and again, growing fuzzier and more frenzied in his lust, pawing and grunting until finally his brain exploded with a sunburst of ecstasy and he collapsed across the damp white and lavender bedclothes. He lolled there, spent but not quite asleep, in the humid air.

After a few minutes of dazed afterglow, Jim reached for the woman, but found himself alone in the bed. Disoriented, he rose and began to dress, but paused when he caught the flecks of gold glittering in his chest and leg hairs. Brushing and plucking at the sparkles only seemed to bury them deeper, and he briefly thought of a shower, but then the first heavy footfall echoed in the hallway outside the door.

Jim scrabbled into his clothes as the weary footsteps plodded towards the room. He was just fixing his belt, and only then realizing how disheveled the bed linens were and how the cloying smell of sex and perfume still hung in the air, when the door opened and a stranger entered.

The man was about Jim's age, maybe a little older. He wore a light jacket, and his cheeks were still pink from the air outside. Without speaking he took in the scene and then raised his hand to his cheek slowly, as if weighed down by the heavy gold ring on his finger. He rubbed the stubble on his jaw, and even in the dim light, his knuckles were obviously darkened and split.

"I'm sorry," Jim sputtered. "I didn't—"

"Don't apologize." The stranger waved Jim off. He unzipped his jacket as he walked to the far window overlooking the street.

"Your wife, though," Jim tried to continue.

Silhouetted in the window frame, the man chuckled. "I'm just a visitor like you."

"What?" Jim asked.

"We're the same," the man said.

Curiosity held Jim. "How so?"

The man turned back to Jim and sighed. He shrugged off his jacket and let it fall to the floor, then began to unbutton his shirt. He spoke as he stripped.

"You and I, we're not happy boys. We're trapped in jobs, lives, marriages"—the now-shirtless man pointed to his ring and then towards Jim's own wedding band—"that pin us and squeeze us. We suffer in silence, always the good guys, but that isn't what men like us are supposed to do, is it? Men sacrifice. They build things."

"Yes. I mean, no." Jim paused at the edge of the bedroom door. The stranger wasn't exactly threatening, but as the man dug one shoe off with his toes and then the other, the air grew thicker.

"Something drew you to this house, right? And when you found it, you found her, too, right?" The man undid his belt and with a single thrust, shucked pants and underwear to the floor. "You came upstairs and you did something bad, didn't you?"

"Yes," Jim whispered, equally mortified and riveted.

"Men build, or men destroy. We proliferate or it consumes us, right?" The naked stranger stretched his arms and then rubbed his bloated stomach. "So maybe what we did wasn't bad. Maybe it was natural. That's how these things work: procreate and provide. When the drives are thwarted, they have to come out somewhere, right? It's just basic survival."

Jim nodded. It was as if this naked man could see into his soul.

"I liked it," Jim said. "I felt like the me I want to be again."

The naked man moved towards Jim, the flab around his midsection and his flaccid penis jiggling with each step. He reached out with his bruised hands, and Jim couldn't move.

"She gave you something, too. You've got it on you now, in you." The man brushed the side of Jim's hair with surprising tenderness. A few specks of gold fell like dandruff to his shirt. "You're going to take it home, to share it with the little lady so that she'll appreciate you and remember how things should be, right?"

Grinning, the man leaned in close enough that Jim could smell his breath like moldy peaches. "So you can be the man of the house again, right?"

With a burst of anger, Jim shoved the man. The stranger stumbled backwards before catching himself, and Jim braced for an attack, but the man just laughed, thin and wheezing. Then he wiped his eyes and turned away.

"I told you we're the same," he said as he waved Jim away and then began to caress the wall. Finding a loose edge in the wallpaper, he gingerly peeled a strip of it from the far corner and then smiled as he pressed a finger against the exposed surface. Jim was going to say something else to challenge the man, but the stranger pulled back his fingers, glistening with a thick and translucent substance, and his nostrils whistled as he inhaled deeply.

Jim turned and fled the grotesque display. By the time he was outside and sparkling faintly beneath the streetlights, however, the encounter was already fading like a bad dream.

He had to get home. It was imperative.

<hr />

Once Laurie hangs up after telling Jim about the procedure, he could stop the car and find somewhere to wait until his mind cleared. He could turn around and go home to prepare an apology or start dismantling the nursery. Instead, he drives in circles while a singular mantra runs its circuit through his wires: *Men build, or men destroy.*

Eventually, he finds the house, but it isn't what he remembered. Instead of the nice suburban cul-de-sac that he dimly recalled, it squats in a mangy lot near an unkempt tree break. For a moment he entertains the hope that he's mistaken, that it's like seeing a friend at a distance, then rushing up only to find a stranger. But there is no mistaking those windows, although now cataracted with grime. That's the same peaked roof that now sags like a battered hat. The front door that had drawn him in like puckered lips now gawps, its steps drooping to the brittle lawn. The little lollipop tree's bare branches shiver like bones.

Jim enters, no longer buoyed along by the heady scent of an ill-timed spring. Everything inside is now either withered and dry or bloated and soft. The kitchen, the living room, the dining room are all in disarray; settling timbers groan amid the echoes of dripping water. Jim can't bring himself to enter the nursery, but a crack in the wilted door reveals that the daffodil walls are now jaundiced. Like an ultrasound, gray water damage and fuzzy constellations of black mold blot out the murals in a static that Jim can't quite penetrate, although he senses movement behind the grit.

The dry, dusty smell he remembered is smothered beneath a floral decay. Gagging in the spore-filled air, Jim's every step up the stairs threatens to press through this false world's soft flesh. The second floor hallway sags like the inside of an intestine, and the carpet squelches as cool water seeps up through his soles and soaks his socks. Doors that had been closed before are now peeling away like scabs, revealed as false fronts covering the rot. The only real door is the one that hangs like a mottled tongue at the hall's end. Jim has nowhere left to go but into the mouth of it.

Inside the master bedroom, the floor and ceiling dip. Strips of wallpaper curl away like ferns to expose globs of paste like thick tears, as if the walls are mourning the tattered violet mass at the bed's stained center. The bedside lamp flickers like a dying firefly and, in the erratic illumination, Jim can see that the purple lump on the bed— the lure that Jim had fallen upon in delusional and ultimately insatiable lust—had always been a trick. He spreads the flesh-heavy cloak into the outline of the woman he thought he had seen, finally comprehending the two-dimensional curves and the flat markings that, in the dimness, he had mistaken for a face. From its back, a thick, limp stem like an umbilicus connects it to the wall.

It's dying, Jim knows. His perfect home is a lie. Like an exotic orchid, some trick of the climate had coaxed it into bloom so that, starving and desperate to propagate, it had called to him. Its time is up, though, and it no more belongs here now than Jim does.

He should go back home, he knows. Back to apologize for the

damage he's done to Laurie and their life together. But even if Laurie could ever forgive him, Jim couldn't admit to her—to anyone—that he had been fooled again. He won't make himself a laughingstock or let her see him as any less of a man than he already is. Destruction flashes across his mind: the wooden bones of this place in flames; the seed of the nursery in Laurie's house gutted to the timbers.

But, even in its degraded state, this house still has its tendrils in him. Even though Jim has failed to spread it, he can't give up on the whole structure and wipe it away, can he? An enormous sadness settles on him. Procreate and provide: the twin objectives that biology and society have conditioned Jim to pursue at all costs. A failure at the former, couldn't he still fulfill the latter?

Behind the curling wallpaper, Jim sees the outlines of others that must have been like him. Beneath the enticing dew drops, where golden motes and black flies stick fast, are greasy shadows of other men who have given themselves to its walls. One mass is still distinguishable as the naked stranger, although what remains of his skin and organs is now translucent as everything but his gold ring is being digested into the boards. Had they—the stranger, Jim, all of them—come back here after failing to thrive or spread, only to find their ideal home dying? Unable to accept their failure, had they traded themselves to preserve its rotting body just a little longer in the vain hope it might one day take root again?

Jim shivers as he strips his clothes off and discards them in a pile on the floor. For a brief moment, a sharp tinge of mint prickles his nose, but then the droplets stick fast and hold Jim upright as he leans against the wall. It's like falling without moving, and all he feels is a warm numbness seeping through his body.

But isn't this what men did? Hadn't someone told him, once, that men make sacrifices? They build things? *Yes, they do*, Jim thinks as he finally slips down, *even if they're ugly and imperfect. Even if they don't completely understand the imperative.*

THE RISING SON

DONNA AND I WEREN'T MARRIED, which is probably just one reason we didn't go up into the sky with most of the other folks in Despin Creek. Donna set to bawling that we'd missed the Rapture, but I wasn't worried.

I'm what you'd call a practical man.

First, I took my guns and, using those, I took other people's guns. Then, with all those guns, I took all the food. With that settled, people started seeing the wisdom of coming to me.

We gated up the town, fenced it in with old cars and construction supplies. We had hard men and loose women, sure, but also doctors and lawyers and teachers and everything. It was just like the old days, but better, because I was in charge.

Because there was enough canned food in the warehouse and soulless animals in the forest to keep everyone fed.

Because if people didn't get with the plan, then I had other practical solutions.

And it was good for a while, until Donna started really showing, and then one day she said, "Baby, I can feel him in my belly. It's like he's lifting me off the ground."

I thought she was referring to the lightness and joys of maternity, but no.

Donna's what you'd call a literal person.

It was in Doc Greenbriar's office, after hours of pushing and swearing, that I heard the pop. I thought maybe the baby's head had cracked Donna's pelvis open like a pecan, but no. It was just our beautiful baby escaping the bounds of his mother.

And rising.

Straight up like a birthday balloon, with a thick wet tether back into Donna's recesses—the only remaining connection to this sinful world.

He was pink and innocent, and I knew that here was my salvation.

Doc Greenbriar's mouth was wide open behind his blue paper mask, eyes on the baby bouncing on the ceiling. He fumbled for his forceps and his scissors, but I slapped his hands away.

"You idiot," I said, grasping the umbilical string connected to my angelic boy. "If you cut that now, he's liable to float away."

Hand over hand, I pulled him down, feeling the pulse still in the cord. It felt strong, alive. Pure. When the baby was in my arms, I wrapped him in my flannel shirt, squeezing him tight. I could still feel him pulling away.

Up.

He was strong.

"What—what—" the doc stuttered.

"This," I said, "means that there ain't no such thing as Original Sin. It means we might all get to Heaven yet."

As I said, I'm a practical man.

So I took the guns and I took the food, and with those I took Doc Greenbriar and Donna and Sandy and Kaitlin and Deidre and Mandy and Heather and two newcomers who wouldn't tell me their names, and this here lawn chair with these eight bungee cords.

And, in just a few more months, my children and I are going to Heaven.

THE BUCHANAN BOYS
RIDE AGAIN

TANNER BUCHANAN IS WAITING OUTSIDE his ground floor apartment at the back of Dewey Court when his old four-by-four finally grinds into the gravel lot with ex-wife Shelly at the wheel. In its past life, Dewey Court was a motor lodge—two stories of long-term stays buried in the woody part of the county. It was never busy, even in its heyday, so when the bypass put it even deeper into the backwater, it was converted into low-cost apartments. It's the kind of place where men like Tanner seem to end up, although on this holiday weekend it's even more deserted than usual.

Sheltered by the overhang of the second-floor walkway, Tanner puts a hand out to feel for rain, but it's still just mist. The truck's window lowers, and Shelly sticks her head out. The paltry light that penetrates the clots of thunderclouds and the dense woods just beyond the lot is too dim for her usual sunglasses, so Tanner can see the pale circles around her eyes.

"Almost didn't find the place," she says. "GPS doesn't like it out here, huh?"

"Number's out front." Tanner points up toward the Dewey Court sign and the apartment's bank of mailboxes back at the top of the steep driveway.

"Way up there, huh?" Shelly tries to smile. "Good thing I brought my truck."

"Your truck." It comes out colder than intended.

Shelly dips back inside, and what's said in the cab is muffled beneath the engine, with only "Have to," "Because," and "Father" bubbling up. Then their son Colin steps out from the truck. He's so thin beneath his overstuffed bag that when he cranes his neck up, he's both an explorer reading the sun and a snail surprised by rain. He is fifteen going on twenty-five going on twelve.

Tanner saunters over to hug his son who, although stiff, doesn't pull away until Tanner plants a kiss on his forehead. He catches a whiff of stale tobacco clinging to Colin's hair, but doesn't mention it.

"Happy birthday, bud," Tanner says.

"Thanks," Colin mutters, and looks away.

Tanner follows Colin's line of sight back to the apartment building. In the apartment beside his, the blinds held open by Tanner's shut-in neighbor snap closed. On the second-floor landing, an eight-year-old dangles his legs off the edge and picks his nose while glaring at Colin.

"Just ignore the peeper and young Turdrow up there," Tanner says.

"His name's Turdrow?"

"Should be. Kid's a real turd."

Colin giggles, light and childish, but he quickly frowns and shrugs it away.

"Thanks for driving him," Tanner says to Shelly. "We got some big plans."

"Nothing too wild, please," she says. "I'll be by tomorrow at nine to pick him up. We've got a bit of a drive ahead."

Tanner watches Colin steal a glance at the phone he slips from his pocket, already counting down the hours.

"You know the Buchanan boys," Tanner says as he grabs Colin by the shoulder without warning and wrestles him into the noogie position. "Always getting into trouble."

In the sudden tussle, Colin drops his phone and, as it clacks against the stones, with a surge of unexpected fervor, he shoves Tanner away. Disgust flits across Colin's face and Tanner briefly gawps, then turns livid.

"This stinks," Colin says as he stoops to retrieve his phone.

When Colin rises, he and Tanner stare at each other in a silent détente until Colin sniffs dramatically.

"I mean, can't you smell it? Like, something rotting."

Tanner squints. He points slowly off into the impenetrable bramble of trunks and dead needles beyond the parking lot. "There's a lake out back."

Shelly breaks in from the sidelines. "Oh? Good fishing?"

The intrusion diverts Tanner's attention from Colin. "Seriously, Shelly? Are you—" He stops himself. "Sorry. No. There's some kind of run-off or drainage problem. Big fish kill."

All three of them are quiet for a moment.

"Well," Shelly finally says. "I better get going. Packing to do."

She puts the transmission in reverse, but hesitates before taking her foot off the brake. She looks at the heavy clouds and towering trees where the thick nests of tent caterpillars hang. Roots climb over the parking lot's rotten timber barriers and towards the rundown building.

"Try not to kill each other before morning." She forces a tight smile. "Please?"

With that she lets up and the truck rolls back across the nearly empty lot. As she pulls out towards the steep drive, she calls back: "Love you."

Tanner almost answers from force of habit, but bites his tongue. Colin just grunts.

***

A doggie bag from Golden Corral, translucent with grease, slides across the backseat of Tanner's Le Sabre and collides with the plastic bag holding a four-pack of toilet paper, two cans of WD-40, and a bottle of Drano. The windshield wipers keep frantic time as Tanner takes another corner on the wet backroads. His face glows green from the dashboard's light; Colin's glows blue from his phone.

"Aren't you going a little fast?" Colin asks without looking up. He thumbs his way down a page of little icons too fast for Tanner's peripheral vision to register.

"Oh, now you feel like talking?" Tanner says. "In words? To me?"

Colin sighs and tucks his phone between his legs. "What do you want me to say?"

"Just some conversation would be nice. I don't get to see you much."

Tanner eases up a little on the gas. The trees surrounding the road open up into a stretch of field, but the driving rain still curtains off the distance. He looks over at Colin, but Colin is looking out into the downpour.

"Can I smoke in here?" Colin asks.

Tanner puts his foot down and beads of rain streak from the windshield. "So you're a smoker now? How old are you?"

"Are you serious?" Colin says. "We just had my goddam birthday dinner."

"Language," Tanner snaps. "I know how old you are. I was being rhetorical."

"Then how old am I?"

"Sixteen."

"Not until tomorrow." Colin leans back, arms crossed.

"That's what I meant." The car is flying through another tree cluster. A skin of fallen leaves covers the asphalt and obscures the yellow lines. A few broken branches lie in the opposite lane like shaggy beasts in ambush.

"Is that a no?" Colin asks.

"No," Tanner says.

"No, it's not a no? Or no, I can't smoke?"

"It's bad for you," Tanner says.

"I learned by watching you." Colin picks his phone back up and thumbs it on again. "I'm a visual learner."

"Well, I've quit," Tanner says. "So learn that."

Colin mutters something that the wipers and the ricochet of rain conceal.

"Come again?" Tanner asks.

"I said, are we almost back to your place?"

"Yeah."

"Good," Colin says. "I have to pee. It's so far away, no wonder nobody wanted to stay there."

Tanner slams on the brakes and Colin jerks forward, choked briefly by the seatbelt. He opens his mouth, but Tanner's reflection in the windshield, the wipers' furor just beyond, silences him. They're at the crest of the apartment's driveway, next to the bank of mailboxes and weather-beaten Dewey Court sign.

"Do you think I want to live here?" Tanner twists his head like an owl as he unclips his mailbox key from the ring in the ignition. He cranks down the window and leans out to open his cubby. "Here in the woods, next to a shitty lake that floods whenever it rains?"

"No."

"No. But it's a sacrifice I make so that I can pay for you. Your clothes, your house. School. Cigarettes. Your cellphone." He shakes his head. "You're spoiled."

"I'm sorry, Dad," Colin says. "Really. Look, I'll put the phone away."

Tanner retrieves a stack of junk mail all addressed to "Current Resident" or "Our Friend at Dewey Court." He sighs.

"Never mind." Tanner hands Colin the wet papers. "Speaking of cellphones, does yours actually get reception out here? Mine doesn't."

"Barely."

"Can I see?" Tanner holds out his hand, and Colin hands it over. "See? Just one bar."

"Good," Tanner says. "Then you won't miss it until morning."

He tosses the phone in the mailbox, twists the lock closed, and the Le Sabre is already splashing through the growing puddle at the driveway's bottom before Colin can begin cursing.

Colin stands in the bathtub, wearing yellow dishwashing gloves and a pair of Tanner's oversized galoshes as protection from the inch of sediment-hazy water that has gurgled up from the drain. The bottle of Drano waits for him on the tub's edge, but for now he holds the barbed length of a red plastic drain snake and stares at the brown water. Next to him, Tanner sits on the closed toilet lid, a fishing reel on a towel in his lap as he tests the spool and the bail arm. They're a little grungy, so he gives it all a spritz of WD-40 and tries again.

"Why do I have to do this?" Colin asks. "I've never used the tub."

"I haven't hardly, either," Tanner says. "But part of being an adult is learning to take care of things. Besides, I'm working on this reel so we'll be able to take a trip up Despin Creek next month."

"Ugh," Colin grunts. When Tanner looks up at him, Colin points to the drain. "I can see the clumps of hair waving at me."

Tanner draws out the fishing line from the spool, then reels it back and nods in satisfaction at the whir. He puts it down on the counter and picks up a fishing knife, its blade rusted by years of trout guts. Another spray of WD-40, and he sets to rubbing off the oxidization with a stained rag.

"You don't even have this much hair," Colin says.

Tanner tries to hide his smile. "Probably here long before us, but it's our problem now. Plumbing's shot, and the rain backs it up worse than usual."

Colin looks down at the ill-fitting rubber boots swallowing his ankles. "I'm afraid I'm going to slip."

"You can use my hip waders if you need more coverage," Tanner offers.

"I don't need your fancy pants," Colin says. "Can't I just stand, you know, on the floor?"

"Stubborn clogs demand a direct angle of attack."

"Fine." Colin resigns himself and crouches down. "But I'm going to need a smoke after this."

"Your health isn't up for negotiation."

Above them, the ceiling shakes as someone stomps in time to the booms of televised explosions. Colin looks up, and Tanner shakes his head.

"Turdrow," Tanner sighs.

"That's a big noise for a small kid." Colin rolls his eyes as he threads the drain snake down into the clog.

"Mmhmm. Up to all hours."

"Have you ever talked to his parents?"

"If they were around to talk to," Tanner shrugs as he rubs the fishing knife, "I probably wouldn't have to."

"How do I do this?" Colin asks.

Without looking, Tanner answers: "Just give it a yank."

Colin plants his feet and, with a mighty pull, rips the drain snake out, the tip swinging with matted hair, grey soap scum, and indistinguishable mush embedded throughout. Colin stumbles, and both Buchanans gag at the sudden putrid reek.

Tanner scrambles to put down the knife and WD-40, but they clatter to the floor. The reel falls, too, and he leaps to avoid it hitting his toes. Colin is waving the clump of muck at arm's length as brown water splatters the floor and the shower mat.

"What do I do?" Colin gasps. "Oh, shit."

"Language, dammit!" Tanner rips the plastic liner from the trash can by the toilet and holds it out. He grunts as Colin shakes the detritus into the bag, then closes it quickly, the smell somewhat trapped.

"Oh God," Colin says. "That's awful."

Before Tanner can speak, a loud bang shakes the bathroom wall that he shares with the peeping old man next door. Tanner smacks the wall hard enough to shake the mirror in reply.

"Jesus, Colin." Tanner turns back. "You can't just panic. You need to have a plan."

"Panic?" Colin asks. "You were the one dropping things and yelling."

Tanner scoops up the fishing reel assembly to examine it for damage, his criticism unimpeded. "And you have to use steady pressure. Not just yank it."

"But you— Do you want to do this?" Colin asks.

"Are you being smart?"

"No. I'm just a visual learner."

The bail arm on the reel is bent, the bathroom stinks, and Turdrow is stomping above. Colin is standing in a disgusting tub that still won't drain, wobbling in Tanner's ill-fitting boots, apparently incapable of performing even the simplest task. Tanner opens his mouth to say something bad, maybe even something he can't take back.

A bang from the neighbor's wall cuts him off.

"Goddammit!" Tanner's knuckles dent the plaster in violent response. The banging on the other side intensifies, rising in a fevered response before it abruptly stops. Tanner turns around just quickly enough to catch Colin cowering before the boy ducks back down, all his attention on the impacted drain.

"Colin," Tanner tries, "I didn't—"

Another bang cuts him off.

Tanner's anger carries him outside and to his neighbor's door, but it abandons him there. The rain pours unabated just beyond the shelter of the second-story walkway and the gutters are gurgling. The almost-empty parking lot is a stew of mud and gravel where clumps of spiky vegetation float across puddles like drowning rats. Slug trails glisten along the windows, and the moisture seems to have revived every species of lichen and creeper as vegetal threads snake across the brick wall.

The lights are on inside the old man's apartment, but there's no television and no voices. The thumping in the back of the apartment is still audible, although slower and heavier. Tanner knocks, almost politely, on the door. No answer.

Tanner tries the knob. It's locked, of course, but the doors here are just as cut-rate as everything else. He slips one of his expired credit cards from his wallet and jimmies the lock. Fortunately, Dewey Court doesn't have deadbolts.

Once inside the apartment, the odor is so unbearable that Tanner slips his shirt over his nose as a makeshift ventilator. Beyond the unwashed dishes and Ben Gay that he expected of an elderly shut-in, the stench of stagnant water and decay is overwhelming.

"Hello?" he calls out, but there's no answer. As Tanner approaches the half-open bathroom door, the smell takes on a new density, overwhelming his t-shirt filter. Close enough now to make out the striped leg of his neighbor's pajamas, Tanner can see that he's bent over, head down in the sink and arms limp. The sprawl of toiletries evidences a distressed flailing, but, knees buckled, somehow still he remains upright. It's as though his head were glued in place, but when Tanner peers over his neighbor's back, he can only see his dark, greasy hair.

Then the hair pulses. It relaxes, and the neighbor slumps; then it pulls tighter and his forehead smacks against the porcelain. In that moment, Tanner can see that not only is the hair coming out of the drain, but it's trying to pull the old man in.

Without a second thought, Tanner tries to pull the old man upright by his shoulders, but the tendrils from the drain are too strong. He instinctively grabs a clump of the greasy black strands, but falls back howling as they burn his flesh. Like a Portuguese man o' war Tanner once stepped on while fishing, the sick agony of neurotoxin sears into his skin.

"Dad?" Colin shouts, muffled, through the wall.

"Stay there!" Tanner looks around the bathroom, frantic, for any kind of tool. Then he sees the tub and that same inch of stagnant water that Colin's standing in just a wall away. Curlicues of dark hair swirl up from the tub drain, spinning like lures as they break the surface.

Tanner hooks his arms around the old man, and this time plants a foot against the wall. With a mighty shout, he puts his back into it. There's a half-moment of resistance and then they fly backwards, Tanner crashing into the towel rack as he cushions the old man.

"Hey," Tanner says, struggling to rise from beneath the other. "Get up."

Tanner rolls the old man off, and then he can see why he hadn't responded. The old man's face is laid bare, muscles dripping with corrosive goo. Ping-pong ball eyes stare and Chiclet dentures grin at Tanner. Over in the sink, there's the glug and scuff of flesh being sucked into the drain.

***

Tanner hurls himself back into his apartment with enough force that the doorknob cracks the plaster. Shouting for his son, he runs through the living room/kitchenette and slides into the bathroom where Colin stands in the tub, frozen like a frog in a flashlight. His mouth agape, still wearing the oversized boots and dishwashing gloves, the red plastic drain snake droops in Colin's hand.

"Get out!" Tanner shouts.

"What?" The drain by Colin's feet gurgles. "What ha—"

With a squick, a whip of hair shoots from the water and lashes the drain snake's tip. The Buchanan men watch in horror as the black strands split and branch to climb the tool's serrated teeth. Then the hair climbs Colin's gloved fingers, his wrist.

"What the fuck?" He tries to pull away, but his loose footing gives and he slips in the murky water. The force on the other end reels him, splashing, towards the drain.

Tanner grabs the fishing knife from the floor. Its blade still glistens from the WD-40 as he hacks at the strands emerging from the drain. They snap like fishing lines stretched too taut, and Colin tumbles out onto the floor.

"Get it off!" Colin swings his hand, but the filaments are stuck fast to the rubber glove and the snake. The rancid clump is dripping something more acrid than dirty water, so Tanner grabs the closest towel and wraps it around the snake and his son's hand. He peels off the whole contaminated apparatus and tosses the bundle into the tub.

"Don't let it touch you." Tanner rubs the scarlet lines across his palm and feels the shiver of the poison again. "It burns."

"What was—Oh, shit."

More hairs creep like vines over the lip of the bathroom sink behind Tanner. Across the counter, onto the mirror, up the wall, the glistening fibers are reaching out like fingers.

"Be very, very care—" Tanner begins, but Colin has already opened the bottle of Drano. He scrambles past Tanner and sloshes it all into the sink without looking in. The hairs along the wall writhe, and Colin falls back just as the wispy threads flail toward his face. They miss, spasm, and then fall limp.

"Wow," Tanner says, still holding the knife.

"Yeah," Colin says.

"Good job."

"Thanks."

Tanner takes a breath. "Let's run?"

Colin nods. "Yeah."

So they run. Heedless of the downpour, they flee the apartment, splash through the parking lot, dive into the Le Sabre, and have the engine and headlights on before fully grasping the severity of their situation. All around, the ground writhes with tendrils of hair. Matted bolls of every size, from thumb-length to largemouth bass, inch across the ground, up the walls, even upside down along the overhangs. They trail shimmering mucus as they elongate and contract. Spindles of lank hair periodically waft in the air like serpents sniffing.

"Jesus Christ," Tanner whispers. He guns the engine, but the lot is a soup and the Le Sabre's front wheels squeal before finding traction. Fighting for every inch, the car gets them around the corner of the building, but then it's hopeless. The bottom of the steep driveway is a lake, and a silver Volvo is already stuck nose-first in the sludge. There's no path around that isn't flooded or obstructed by trees.

"We'll just call for help," Tanner says. "Give me your phone."

Colin shakes his head, hyperventilating.

"Now," Tanner shouts.

Colin points out of the windshield, past the frantic wipers and the pouring rain, to the mailbox at the top of the drive. His phone is right where Tanner locked it away.

"Goddammit!" Tanner slams his head against the steering wheel. When he lifts it up, Colin is on the verge of tears.

"It's okay," Tanner says. "You just wait here. I'll run up and get it, okay?"

As he says this, the driver's door of the half-submerged Volvo opens and a woman climbs out. She sinks up to her calves in the muck as she struggles towards the Buchanans' car and waves in a desperate signal. Tanner honks to let her know that he sees her.

From above, a dark web falls across the woman like a veil. Her eyes roll back, her arms jerk, and for a second she hangs like a marionette held in dead hands. Then a black dog's worth of fur plummets from unseen branches above and crushes the woman face-first into the dirty water.

"We have to help her." Colin lunges for the door, but Tanner grabs his shirt.

Beyond the comparative safety of the Le Sabre, more furry things are already crawling towards the puddle. In just a few seconds, the woman is buried under so many strands of toxic hair that she looks like a lump of dead pine needles. All around them, the shadows and tall trees are alive with danger.

Tanner lets go and puts the Le Sabre into reverse. "It's not a negotiation."

"We have to try," Colin sputters, but his fight has gone.

∽

Dewey Court's power went out twenty minutes ago and, although the rain is letting up, the heavy clouds beyond the trees still choke out all but the faintest moonlight. Inside Tanner's apartment, a menagerie of candles—long-stemmed, tea light, air-freshening—flicker around the Buchanans huddled on the couch. Around them, crude precautions have been set: the tub drain is covered with a frying pan and a twenty-five pound dumbbell on top; the bathroom sink is jammed with a red t-shirt, its end protruding slightly like a tongue; the toilet, a pair of jeans; the kitchen sink, both dishrags. The windows and door edges are smothered under duct tape. Tanner and Colin are as sealed as they can be.

On the coffee table before them, a creature—dead, disfigured by Drano, and snaked from the bathroom sink—lies on a dinner plate like a regurgitated meal. Tanner's cellphone, its bars of reception replaced by a prominent NO SIGNAL, provides impotent blue light as he prods the creature with a fork.

"A worm, maybe?" Tanner pushes aside a patch of fur that wasn't ruined by the caustic unclogging agent and reveals reticulations. "But hairy, obviously."

Tanner twirls the thing's sticky tendrils around his fork tines like angel hair pasta. The strands connect into a proboscis-like appendage that extends from an opening near its puckered sphincter of a mouth. "Have you heard of ribbon worms? Those have—"

"Dad," Colin interrupts. "Unless this is getting us out of here, please stop."

Tanner lays the fork down. "I know this is scary," he says, "but we're safe now. We're sealed up."

As if in emphasis, the pipes in the walls groan. Tanner and Colin both shiver at the sound of dense bodies undulating around their sanctuary.

"We're sealed up, all right," Tanner repeats. "And your mom will be here first thing in the morning. She'll call for help. We'll leave in my—her truck." He pats Colin on the shoulder. "We just have to sit tight."

"I can't believe I'm going to die here," Colin says.

"No one's going to die," Tanner says.

"No one else, you mean."

Tanner ignores him, but Colin continues.

"I didn't even want to come here." Colin pulls a soft pack of American Spirits and a white Bic from his pocket. Before Tanner can say anything, Colin lights one. He holds it pinched between thumb and forefinger, like a child sipping a juice box, as he takes a weak drag.

"Put that out," Tanner says. "There's no smoking allowed inside."

Colin laughs himself into a coughing fit. "You're not getting your deposit back."

"Those things will kill you," Tanner says.

Colin points his cigarette at the plate holding the half-melted slug. "That's the thing that's going to kill me."

"Nothing's going to kill you."

Colin snorts. "Great. So you're going to protect me from the mess you got me into."

"I didn't do this, Colin," Tanner says. "And put that out."

Colin grinds the cigarette out beside the creature.

"I know this is tough," Tanner tries to keep an even tone, "but you're not being fair to me."

"What are you talking about, 'fair to you'? If you wanted to protect me, you should have been there for me."

Tanner clenches his jaw. He knows he shouldn't speak when he's upset, but it's too late. "Do you know how much I sacrifice for you?"

"Nobody wants your sacrifice!" Colin jumps up from the couch. "If you couldn't protect me by being with me somewhere better, why couldn't you just leave me alone?"

Tanner stands, fists clenched. Colin leans in, chin forward. The walls around them pound like a heart against the clotted valves, the pressure rising as each Buchanan silently dares the other.

A scream from the floor above pierces the room.

"Turdrow." Tanner grabs his fishing knife. "Stay here."

Tanner moves towards the door, but Colin dives on him to wrestle him back. "Don't leave me!" Colin shouts.

"I have to help Turdrow." Tanner struggles against his son. "I'll come back."

Colin lets go. "I've heard that before."

Tanner looks around at the clogged drains and taped windows. Upstairs is a sobbing child, but before him is his son, and they both know well enough how Tanner's best intentions go awry. Still, he thinks, it isn't fair to force him to make this choice.

"Fine, I'll stay," Tanner says. "We'll just hope Turdrow makes it out. Is that what you want?"

He drops back onto the couch and puts the knife down. Around them, the pipes are gurgling. Above them, Turdrow is crying.

"No," Colin says. He squares his scrawny shoulders. "I meant I'm going with you."

"No," Tanner says. "I won't leave you, but I won't let you leave, either, so whatever happens to Turdrow you can blame on me, okay?"

Colin throws his hands up. "Stop your stupid martyr act!"

Tanner throws his hands up too. "What do you want from me?"

Colin squints. He takes a moment to weigh his words. "To be less of an impossible asshole. And to treat me like an adult."

"You're only fifteen."

"Sixteen." Colin picks up Tanner's useless phone and shows him the time—12:17 a.m.

Tanner bites back his smile. "When did you get so damn stubborn?"

"I told you, I learn from example."

Tanner shrugs. He sighs. "Well, let's go then."

"Okay," Colin says, "but instead of rushing off like usual, let's make a plan."

THE BUCHANAN BOYS RIDE AGAIN

Above them, Turdrow's frantic wail jumps an octave. Tanner reaches for his knife, but Colin grabs his father's wrist, hard.

"Not a negotiation," Colin says.

On the second-floor landing, outside Turdrow's apartment door, Tanner and Colin make their final preparations. Tanner wears his overall-style PVC hip waders and a light raincoat with the arms layered in Saran wrap until they shimmer like ice. Colin stills wears the oversized galoshes, but has added Tanner's knee-length heavy rain slicker. They both wear yellow dishwashing gloves.

Tanner sprays them down with a can of WD-40 as if it were aerosol sunscreen—hoods, torsos, arms, feet. A lot on the feet. They glisten as Tanner puts the WD-40 back into his overstuffed fanny pack next to his phone, his fishing knife, and his keys. He fumbles around inside it before pulling out his credit card. "Ready?"

Colin nods. Tanner pops the door lock.

Inside, it's worse than they had imagined. The floor writhes with greasy sheets of hair. The walls and ceiling appear to have been spackled with the crud snaked from drains. All the shaggy strands that drape the furniture shiver. Moist, furry bodies leave lines of luminescent slime over every surface.

Tanner's first tentative footstep sinks among the carpet of creeping tendrils, but the thick layers of WD-40 and rubber keep them from gaining hold. Tanner points down and Colin pumps his fist as if to say, "I told you." Together they enter the living room, but it's clear from a glance that Turdrow isn't there.

Turdrow's muffled sobs grow louder as they reach the hallway that leads to the bedrooms. The worms' groping hairs slip off of Tanner's legs and arms as he gently opens the door. Enough illumination escapes from a hair-choked, battery-powered Donald Duck nightlight by the entry for Tanner and Colin to see the room, but their survey reveals only a bed, a small desk in the corner, a wicker laundry basket, and a few toys, all smothered under the viscous mat of fur. The only sound is the susurrus of the worms.

"Hello?" Tanner whispers.

GORDON B. WHITE

The laundry basket's lid opens just a crack, and two frightened eyes peer out. The motion alerts the creatures, though, and the layer of toxic strands grows thicker as the slugs swarm over one another towards the motion. The lid slams closed.

Tanner turns to his son. "Ready for the Buchanan Boys to ride again?"

Colin shakes his head.

"Me either. But let's do it."

As nimbly as his greased-up rubber pants allow, Tanner lopes across the room. The desk wobbles as Tanner clambers onto it and pulls his cellphone from his fanny pack. Although it still defiantly proclaims to have NO SIGNAL, Tanner has secured it with duct tape to a thick fishing line. Since his rubber gloves impede his thumbs, Tanner uses his nose to punch in the security code—today's date, of all things—and opens the timer app, already set for fifteen seconds. A gentle tug to make sure it's secure, then Tanner boops the start button and gives the phone a slow underhand pitch towards the basket where Turdrow hides. It hits the roiling hairball with a gentle thump.

Twelve long seconds later, the alarm goes off.

Vibrating and squealing, the lure of the phone is irresistible. Tanner trawls it across the floor, and the predatory carpet opens behind it as the worms and their feelers give chase. Colin wastes no time—as soon as the path is clear, he makes his move. Tanner watches his son pull the little boy from the basket and hold him to his chest, drawing him as far as possible beneath the slicker's wing. His heart swells with a pride he's never felt for himself as he watches them escape into the hall.

Now Tanner has reeled the phone over to the desk's edge, and the tumbleweed of poisonous tendrils has followed. This might almost be heroic, Tanner thinks, as far as ways to go out. But only almost. Instead, he leaps off the desk, hits the bed feet-first, and bounces out into the hallway. He is an eagle soaring, until he hits the ground and his ankle twists, sending him careening into the wall and shattering a hanging portrait of the Turdrow family.

Tanner's crash landing aggravates the worms, and now the whole

THE BUCHANAN BOYS RIDE AGAIN

living room—floor, walls, ceiling—is churning in agitation. Colin runs with Turdrow towards the front door, and Tanner limps to follow. Starving hair climbs like kudzu and drips like Spanish moss, but the thick rubber pants, Saran-wrap gauntlets, and WD-40 keep them from ensnaring him as Tanner kicks and paws through the tangled mass.

Colin is already outside and, with a mighty push, so is Tanner. With Colin under Turdrow's weight and Tanner on a sprain, they hobble as fast they can to the staircase and down the stairs. Tanner fumbles at the fanny pack, but the kerfuffle has twisted it around behind him, so he unclips it just in case they need its provisions one last time. They're just on solid ground with safety in sight when Tanner's leg goes out from under him and the fanny pack flies off into the darkness as he smacks face-first onto concrete.

He shakes away the blood and stars, only to see that a net of hair engulfs the left leg of his waders from shin to toe, braiding back into a thick rope that runs across the lot. Frozen, Tanner stares as a bristling slug the size of a bear lumbers out from the shadows and into the muddy lot next to the Le Sabre. The monster's crested back reaches the car's hood, and two eyestalks with bulging iridescent orbs sway above the giant's slavering mouth and lasso appendage. It blinks its moist lashes as it looks at Tanner; then, with a great slurp, the line goes taut as the abomination sucks him in.

"Dad!" Colin drops Turdrow to his feet. "Stay here," he warns the boy, and then runs to where Tanner scrabbles in the muck. The commotion is attracting the smaller slugs, and a wave of dark hair spreads across the ground as they inch towards him, their whipcords flailing through the drizzle.

"I got you," Colin says as he grabs his father's arms and digs his heels in. The oversized galoshes sink into the mud, but the Buchanans' combined weight stops the gargantuan slug's pull. With a grunt, Colin takes a step back and Tanner pushes with his free leg and, at the other end of the dripping cord, the slug slides just an inch beneath their unified strength.

Tanner laughs. "We got it!"

The slug bats its glowing eyes in frustration and, like a whip-crack, curls its back body around the Le Sabre's rear wheel. Looped around its counterweight, the monster halts Colin and Tanner's progress.

Tanner moans. "We don't got it."

With renewed effort, the slug pulls, gurgling as Tanner and Colin slide slowly back across the mud. The smaller ones' tendrils lick up against Tanner's waders.

"Run," Tanner yells over his shoulder as the first worms crawl onto his lower legs. "Take Turdrow and lock yourselves in."

Behind them, Tanner hears an outsized splashing and then a second, smaller pair of hands grabs him. It's Turdrow, come to join the tug of war.

"I told you to stay back," Colin says between gritted teeth.

"I'm helping," Turdrow says.

And, surprisingly, he is. As the three of them pull, Tanner feels his joints beginning to separate under the strain, but they've stopped moving forward. The dark shapes of the smaller slugs are drawing in, but the humans have managed to arrest their slide towards the giant's trembling gullet and rolling eyes. Its grip around the Le Sabre might even be loosening.

Turdrow gives a cheer. "We got—"

"Don't say it!" Tanner and Colin yell, but it's too late. The gigantic slug's eyestalks retract into its fur, squinting and trembling as if in deep concentration. Then, with an audible pop, glistening black spikes as thick as pencils burst from its sides with enough force to not only anchor it to the ground, but to puncture the Le Sabre's tires and doors. The wounded car gives a dying hiss as the air escapes and liquid drips from beneath.

Turdrow lets go of Tanner and runs.

Tanner kicks like a one-legged mule, trying to shed the fast-ascending smaller slugs from his legs. The giant worm's spines quiver in anticipation and its bulging eyes bobble in delight. The gaping pink maw glistens as the thing contracts its single giant muscle, and Colin slips in the mud and falls so that now he holds Tanner in his lap as the slug reels them both in.

THE BUCHANAN BOYS RIDE AGAIN

"Colin Morgan Buchanan!" Tanner's voice cracks. "You let me go this instant."

Colin ignores him. He's truly as stubborn as his father.

"Please," Tanner says through tears. "Just save yourself."

Colin is crying, too, as he strains to hold on. "I told you, Dad. I don't want your goddam sacrifice. I just want you."

"I love you," Tanner sobs.

"I, I lo—"

"Hey," Turdrow interrupts from behind. "Look."

Tanner can't turn around to see, but Colin's grip slackens for just a second.

"Never mind," Colin says abruptly. "I'm letting go."

"Wait! I—" Tanner begins, but Colin drops him and rolls out from underneath his father, standing just as Turdrow reaches into the retrieved fanny pack and lobs him the can of WD-40. Colin snatches it out of the air like a magician and, with unnecessary flourish, pulls his cigarette lighter from beneath the raincoat. With a hiss and a flick of the Bic, Colin combines his implements into a flamethrower that lights the lot with a crimson burst. The heat and proximity makes Tanner sweat despite the drizzle.

Colin waves the flame over the smaller slugs that crawl towards them on the ground. Their long tendrils curl with the sharp scent of burning hair as their fat bodies sizzle and pop, squealing as their innards steam. The giant one pauses for a moment, understandably confused by the sudden burst of light and heat, and in that confusion Turdrow rushes to Tanner's side, brandishing the fishing knife. He begins to saw at the shoulder straps of Tanner's waders, but Tanner takes the knife from him to do it faster.

The slugs on the waders are crawling towards Tanner's face, and the first of the hairs extend over his chest, lapping at his exposed neck. He screams as the neurotoxin burns his skin.

"Get them off!" Tanner yells, still sawing frantically. Turdrow swings the empty fanny pack at the closest one and bats it off into the darkness, but there are too many, their nest of stinging hairs too close.

"Hold on!" Colin yells, and a burst of flame sweeps across

Tanner's legs. The furry worms flail as they catch and burn, but their thick secretions hold the flaming bodies in place. The PVC of the waders is beginning to melt and singe even as the remaining slugs, too damp or too far away to burn now, squirm up Tanner's thighs.

"Again!" Tanner shouts. His knife finishes severing one shoulder strap and the tension releases, but just a little. The giant slug's coil is wrapped too tight, so Tanner saws at the last restraint.

Colin rattles the can. Only a few drops left.

"Again!" Tanner repeats.

Colin gives one last flick of the lighter and the can sputters as he transforms the last bit of juice into a fireball that scorches the last slugs. Their oily smoke permeates the air, but their pyrotechnic death throes have fully set the waders on fire now, and the outer layer is in flames. Colin throws the empty can away and grabs Tanner under the armpit of his free side. The giant slug gives a final reckless heave to dislodge this troublesome prey.

The last shoulder strap gives way beneath the blade. The flaming pants fly towards the giant slug and slap it across the face. Impaled on the monster's spikes and wrapped around its eyestalks, the pants cling tight to its face even as the monster bellows and thrashes. Tanner, Colin, and Turdrow stare from the mud as the conflagration spreads and the monstrous thing twists beneath the sheet of fire.

"Holy cow," Turdrow gasps. Then he sniffs the air. "Do you guys smell something?"

Colin sniffles. Tanner wrinkles his nose. Their eyes go wide.

"Run!" Colin and Tanner shout as one, just as the flaming behemoth staggers towards them. They scramble back to Tanner's apartment and slam the door behind them just as the flames consuming the monster's fur spark the trail of pungent gasoline leading back to where the worm's spines had wounded the Le Sabre.

The resulting explosion blasts the creature against the apartment's outside wall with a heavy squelch that shakes the windows.

~~~

THE BUCHANAN BOYS RIDE AGAIN

Back inside Tanner's apartment, the burning Le Sabre provides enough of a cozy glow through the windows to see that Tanner, Colin, and Turdrow look as bad as the giant slug's roasting remains smell. His pants a casualty, Tanner's soggy briefs and damp socks make his pale legs look almost scrawny. Turdrow is a mudball staining the couch. Colin sprawls on the floor, soaking through the shag.

Tanner risks opening the bathroom door just wide enough to grab towels. He throws one to Colin and one to Turdrow.

"I shouldn't have put you at risk," Tanner says as he dries his legs.

Colin ruffles his own hair with his towel. "It's okay. It worked out."

"Thanks to me," Turdrow says from his puddle on the couch.

"Thanks to all of us," Tanner says. "But still. I shouldn't have done that."

"It was fine," Colin answers.

"It was too much. It was—"

"It was pretty damn cool." Colin stands and digs the soaked pack of cigarettes from his pocket. He tosses the ruined smokes onto the table next to the dead slug. "I mean, the Buchanan Boys make a pretty good team."

If he were wearing pants, Tanner would have hugged his son. Instead, he just smiles and says, "We did kick some ass, didn't we?"

"Some damn ass," Turdrow adds, clearly relishing the adult talk.

"Damn ass, indeed." Tanner lets himself smile. "But now let's just sit tight until—"

Outside, a scream pierces the night—another neighbor pleading for help.

Tanner looks at Colin, then Turdrow. Colin nods. Turdrow picks up the fishing knife and swings it wildly through the air.

Colin tosses his towel onto the counter. "I'll grab the other can of WD-40 and you put on some pants, Dad. This looks like another job for the Buchanan Boys."

"And Ryan!" Turdrow shouts.

Tanner and Colin turn in unison. "Who?"

OPEN FIGHT NIGHT AT THE DIRTBAG CASINO

WHEN I OPEN MY EYES, Friday night is already spreading above this pinch of an alley like a bruise beneath a fingernail. A quick check-in reveals a few more scrapes and a few less teeth than the last go-round, but I get that familiar tremor of anticipation just before the streetlights start popping on like flash bulbs for the knockout punch. I make a bead for the main drag to get my bearings and then I'm off, babies, off to the fights. Because it's Friday night, and tonight's the night I'm finally gonna kill Tommy Marone.

The rabble call him Tommy the Truck. A big bastard, hands like dumpsters and a porta-john face pasted over with a regular city transit map of scars. A lesser Catskills of contusions and dents crosses the top of his skull. He's not pretty, but he's the champ down at the Casino, and it isn't a kissing booth they're running.

It takes more than a few seasick stumbles to get these legs beneath me, but that's the story just about every Friday. Another spin of the wheel. Another down, another out, another chance next week. Just wake up, readjust, reorient, and head back on down to the Casino.

It isn't really a casino, although they probably got marked cards and stepped-on cocktails on the other side of the chicken wire that separates spectators from the Pit. I don't recall ever being on that side. No, I know the back door and the meat locker and the doorway out to the Pit itself. And, babies, do I know the Pit—that 15-foot circle of plywood, extra-absorbent kitty litter, and enough blood to choke a horse. You know, if horses drank blood.

GORDON B. WHITE

I also know there are two ways out of the Pit. First is upright, through the doors that the Truck comes in, back into his green room and who knows what luxuries. Other way out, you go lying down. I've never been the former and as many times as I've been the latter, it isn't exactly a thing that a body remembers.

Gotta stay positive, though. Tonight's still a chance, even if I'm starting to realize this old body has seen better days. There's a hitch in the step that I can't quite figure, and the winking scabs across these arms are aching for something more than sweet revenge. No, sir, not a looker and maybe not, as show time approaches, enough to get it done.

Goddam.

But it's Friday night and there ain't shit else to do. Besides, this might still be the night I get one over on the Truck. You never know at the Casino, right? It's that chance that gets me going, that makes every turn downright intoxicating.

Before I can get in, though, a rundown of my pockets turns up empty and if I know Don, the Friday night backdoor man, just getting in, especially in this shape, is gonna take some extra grease. So I stop by the alley catty-corner from the Casino to hit up this loose brick that serves as my personal bank and concierge. It's near this filthy ethnic restaurant that must be real authentic, since it always smells like garlic and dirt herbs back here. Sometimes it makes me hungry, sometimes it makes me sick, but I've never been by here other than on Friday and my Fridays are always booked.

Just a quick stop to jiggle the masonry out of joint and make a deposit if I wake up flush, or a withdrawal if I'm broke. Tonight I notice, as I pull out the wadded bills from their hidey-hole, that the till is looking a bit undernourished. Well, I'd make a note to refill it, but that's not as much up to me as I'd like. All a matter of chance, really.

The Casino's backdoor is thick and cold and when I give it the old one-two knock, the little peephole slides open to treat me to doorman Don's piggy eyes. They squint almost closed as he gets a whiff of me, even through the metal and the deadbolts.

"Beat it, bum," Don says. "We don't do charity."

"I'm here for the fight," I say. We do this song and dance every week, and this is always my jab.

OPEN FIGHT NIGHT AT THE DIRTBAG CASINO

"Don't know what you're talking about." That's his feint.

"Course you do," I say, throwing it out there. "The old grab and tickle, the punch and scrape." Don's ignorance is a test, some light sparring to keep the jamokes at bay, so I don't mind the give and take.

"No fights here," he says right on cue. "Don't know you or what you're saying."

Now comes the entry fee. I peel out the bills, as smooth as these damn jitterbug hands will let me. Not loving the odds tonight, but this is the game.

"All on me." I push the cash towards the slot. "To kill the Truck." Don backs away just a little, which a passerby might think was due to his delicate sensibilities—or maybe his nose, because Christ, I'm ripe—but we've done this Friday night bob and weave as long as I can remember, so I know what to say next.

"Minus whatever cover you think is fair." That's the 'Open Sesame' that makes Don the genie that grants my wish. The cash disappears and the locks give me a slow applause as Don undoes them, one by one. I take my first, and hopefully not last, victory walk of the evening through the open door.

"Thank you, Don." I doff a pretend cap down into a mock bow.

"How do you dirtbags always know my name," he grumbles.

"It's only me, Don." I hold up my hands in mock surrender, but leave them up so he can pat my body down. Luckily, there's no surprises for us.

Afterwards, he goes to wipe his hands on his pants but stops, disgusted. Instead, he holds them out like dirty diapers, then hooks a thumb off down one of the dim halls. The bare bulbs flicker in their joy to see me again. "Hit the showers, scuzz."

"I know the drill, Don," I say, already on my way.

"How?" There's a sharper edge in his voice than just the weariness I'm used to. "How would you know the drill?"

Maybe I've pushed him too far, come a bit too close to revealing my hand. No sense in jinxing it.

"Sorry, boss," I say. "Just cracking wise."

Don's not the brightest bulb in the shed, but that bit of bow and scrape sets him right. He grunts to let me know it's satisfactory, but, oh, poor Don. If only he knew.

GORDON B. WHITE

Down the hall, into the shower where the water runs black off of me, and then into the meat locker-cum-locker room. A roll of tape and a pair of gym shorts wait for me, so I get dressed and wrap my hands. Sealed away in this pre-fight limbo, waiting for the Pit crew to let me out onto the killing floor, I work myself into God's own frenzy. I swing my arms, stomp my feet and suck in fast, ragged breaths like a bilge pump that sucks up memories out of the deep recesses and spews them all over the locker room's echo chamber.

Sometimes, I can even sift out which ones are mine.

How did I end up here? Why is it that I'm here to kill the Truck? To rip his face off, gouge his eyes out, dig my fingers into the root of his tongue and pull it out and eat it? Well, believe you me, babies, I got a damn good reason, and I got a plan to give it to the Truck just before I burst his eardrums and suck them out of his skull. So don't you worry, you'll all hear it, too.

For now, though, the why isn't as important as the what. I picture every bloody drop of my vengeance, turning the burner under that smoldering anger up to gut-melting, lava-shitting rage. These veins are empty sewer lines, but the bile keeps backing up, churning and roiling, until my kidneys empty all that adrenaline into me at once like the pressure release of the Hoover Dam. My leftover teeth grind against each other until one of them cracks. Panther-pacing the room, when the Pit door opens and that first bit of fluorescence peeks its head around, I burst forth into the light like an avenging angel.

The crowd roars as I enter, those glorious bastards.

There's probably some kind of pre-fight announcement, a pomp to this circumstance that drums the crowd into a frenzy, but it's over by the time they turn me loose. The crew learned long ago to let the Truck have his little moment before they open my door, since I don't tend to do much standing around.

I come careening out and crash into the Truck like an unlicensed cab on the crosstown. He's got size and strength and probably skill, but I got frenzy, babies. Like the man said, I don't know karate, I know psychotic.

Haymakers, rabbit punches, open-hand slaps and elbows and knees, I'm giving him the kitchen sink but he's shaking it off. He laughs, that ugly baby face of his split in pure mirth, the dark stubble of his head making him look like a scrotum. One of my blows catches lucky, though, and splits his big lip in a different way, kissing my fingers red.

"Do you like that?" My smile replaces his. "Does it help you remember?"

But he's got no answer, just roars and lunges. I step back out of what I thought was a grab, but instead he stomps on my foot and a thousand tiny bones all shatter. I'm pinned as his fist clubs down like a lamppost onto my hood, scraping just as much as it bashes, which is a lot. The searing pain opens like a curtain, but the Truck knuckles my gut like pizza dough and the air that comes up brings along equal parts blood and vomit. The Truck grins and shakes his head.

"Don't know what you're talking about." He grips my lower jaw with a hook of a hand, sinking those pliers he calls fingers into the soft parts between tongue and chin. "Maybe you should just shut up."

I wish I had more teeth so I could bite him, but it isn't meant to be. Instead, he digs in and starts pulling, pulling, puts a foot on my chest and then something comes loose and he's made me into a waterfall. Things are going dim as he holds my jaw above his head, the skin flapping off it like a banner.

The crowd roars as I die again. Those bastards.

～

I can't tell you where I go in-between. Somewhere green and bright that sounds like a thousand cars all rushing past me on a freeway. It feels like being in the wake of all these vessels, swaying around and buffeting me, but it's not frightening. I know I can move on whenever I want.

In fact, on the horizon is a speck of blue, just a teardrop, but I know that—if I wanted—I could reach out and touch it and leave this all behind. But I don't. Because there's another Friday every week, babies, so instead I take a swan dive into the traffic and whichever passing car hits me first is the ride I get tonight. My next ticket into the Casino and into the Pit.

Spin the wheel, babies, back to the city and another Friday night to kill or be killed by the Truck.

GORDON B. WHITE

〜

Another Friday and, from the body I'm in, it's ladies' night.

"We don't let dames fight," Don says.

"Why? Ain't this America?"

"Who are you, lady?"

"Fuck your mother," I say, "minus a cover." My money is in Don's hand and the door is open before I can finish my usual repartee. He thumbs towards the shower.

As I'm scrubbing down, I catch a glimpse of myself in the mirror and damn, if I weren't me, the things I'd do to me. Actually, I might even do them to myself as myself, if I had more time, but I'm already in the locker room and the memories are swirling, new ones from this body joining the peanut gallery of all the others, and then the doors are open. In the Pit, though, the catcalls from the weasel crowd are lewd enough to make these ears burn, but I don't give 'em nothing more than I would any other Friday.

Which is everything I got, covered in blood.

I give the Truck a few good claws and he takes them like a gentleman. There's a look in his eye, far away, sad maybe, but a knee to his groin brings him back *tout suite*. He growls, and just a few real punches to the fragile bones of this face put me down. He fishhooks my cheek and tears it wide, splitting my pretty mouth to the cheekbone. The pain is a raggedy thing, but it's this strange feeling of cool air on the exposed gums, something where it has no business being, that's the worst part of it all. Beneath the familiar calls of the crowd, he crushes my throat and the darkness zippers my eyes.

Spin the wheel again, goddam it.

〜

Some nights are clear losers. Sometimes, like the gambler says, you gotta know when to fold them.

Example for you: It's Friday night and I look down at this frail, tiny body, and shit, it can't be more than what, six years old? Seven? There's no way this is getting out of the apartment, much less into the Casino, never mind the Pit.

OPEN FIGHT NIGHT AT THE DIRTBAG CASINO

What a waste, I think, as I look out the bedroom window over the city below and all its tiny lights, blinking on and off like angels getting and losing their wings. A real crying shame, I think, as I undo the child safety bars. But there's nothing to be done.

It's not until I feel the wind pushing past me and see the ground rushing up like the Truck's fists that I realize I don't even know if I was a boy or a girl this time. Wouldn't have mattered, but still, I'm curious.

The blackness bursts from every pore of my body like a new Big Bang, and then it's time again.

～∾～

It's not like I have to keep going back. There isn't some silver tether or ancient curse that binds me to the Pit, that keeps me circling the Truck, throwing body after body against it. That's just me.

In fact, just between us, one time, one Friday, I didn't come down here at all. No, sir. I came to in this nice little house just outside the city. Oh, sure, I could have caught the rail and been at the Casino with time to spare, but as I was getting my shoes on and letting that body guide me to its keys and its wallet, this guy's wife comes home. And, I mean, I'd probably never seen her before, but there was something about her. A way that her red hair set off against her pale skin; a small gap between her teeth; a mole just under her left eye. This accumulation of all these little details reminded me of someone or someones I must have known, because for once I felt like I was home. She smiled when she saw me, and that part of her husband still inside responded, and that part that's always me, always ready to kill the Truck, well, that went quiet, too.

"I'll have dinner ready soon," she said. "Are you going somewhere?"

"No," we said.

We didn't make it to the fights that night. I don't know who, if anyone, knocked on the Casino's door, made their way into the Pit. Whose blood, if any, was spilled that night for the hungry crowd. For a little while, we, I, didn't care.

It was a good, soft weekend. I let the body do its routines, woke up in the morning, went to work on Monday, and I checked out dreaming of the woman waiting for us. That feeling of being somewhere, of being someone with a place to be. It was nice.

But it was boring, too. So boring. By Wednesday we were fighting, by Thursday we were violent, and come Friday morning, I didn't bother showing up for work but got good and drunk and took out all the money I could from our bank account. Friday night, I was back at the door, begging for Don to let me in, give me one more shot at him.

That one went down like the others. Another body crushed under the Truck, but letting me loose, giving me another chance to spin the wheel.

I don't have a way to keep track of how many times we've done this. No bedpost to carve my notches on, no skin of my own to tattoo the names on, or even little score marks. Each time I take a little bit of whoever it was with me, sure, but to separate them out would be like trying to name each grain of sand on a beach. You get to Ricky, Mickey, Dickey, Moe, and you're already tired of it. Can you imagine trying to keep track of all of them? It's hard enough to keep track of my money.

I was a young guy once, had good speed and a decent cross. The Truck took one on the chin, but ended up breaking my elbow. Beat me to death with a useless arm.

I was an old guy, too, with a few bullet scars and a tattoo of an anchor, figured maybe this one had grit that the others didn't. Some I-don't-know-what that might pull us through, but no. The Truck drowned me in my blood through collapsed sinuses.

A businessman. A stripper, one time. A lawyer, a bus driver, more hobos than I'd like to think about. A crowd of bodies of every shape and color and size and disposition, like lemmings herded over a cliff onto the waiting fists of the Truck below. Dashed, damned, destroyed again and again and again until you could fill a tenement block with all the angry ghosts I keep lugging around with me, yelling at me each Friday night in the locker room.

OPEN FIGHT NIGHT AT THE DIRTBAG CASINO

But that's the thing about odds, right, babies? You lose more than you win.

I'll tell you, a real schmuck once said that insanity is doing the same thing, over and over, but expecting different results.

Baloney.

The crock of it is that you can't ever do the same thing again, not really. There are no true mulligans. No do-overs or backsies or rewinding all the way and pressing play to do it again. That really would be crazy.

Instead, every time you do that thing, even if it's again and again, other things are changing. New conditions, different actors, a different time. Hell, you're a different person, too. And the real change, the actual key, is that this as-of-yet immoveable object that keeps meeting your heretofore not-quite-unstoppable momentum, well, every prior action changes that one, too. That's how a trickle of piss carves a canyon. Like each puff of a cigarette, you might hit that one time that the molecules interact just right, or just wrong, and bloom into cancer.

You're never the same train hitting the same wall, the same straw on the same camel's back. Every time is a brand new beginning and a brand new chance at coming out on top.

You just gotta keep spinning, again and again, to see where it lands.

***

Keep spinning and one Friday night, babies, you'll come up a winner. A real winner this time—young, muscular, arms like suspension bridge cables. So much hell-on-legs that the guy who replaced Don—Thom or Jones or something—doesn't even want to let you in.

Sure, it takes a while, and by the time I get there, the crowd around the Pit is a shadow of what it was in its heyday. But those real ones, those true believers, they'll holler for the punch and scrape, the old grab and tear, just as much as ever. It's us old gamblers that keep things running, keep things going.

And when the Truck comes out tonight, oh, babies, I can see the fear in his eyes. He's got this haunted look, like the broken windows of an empty house before the wrecking ball comes.

It's a fight in name only. Maybe all these years of subpar bodies have weakened him, made him too used to crushing housewives and deadbeats and ordinary people. I must have finally tired him out killing half the city, because I get a few good cracks in and he can barely put his hands up.

I bend a few of his fingers the wrong way until they give. One of his shoulders goes *pop* real loud and then hangs loose. He gets a good taste of my knuckles and then an up-close view. Somewhere after the first minute, he seems to give up and just take it.

Oh, I am enjoying this.

"Just do it," he finally says, rolling his neck up as an offering. His pale eyes tremble behind his red mask. "I've been waiting."

The crowd of people is muttering, not cheering, but my head full of ghosts—all those drops of water that wore away this mountain of a man—they're angry. Is this it, they're saying, this old man? His hair is gray and his limbs are soft. This is what you did it to all of us for? For this broken-down thing?

Shut up, though, babies; shut up and you'll see.

"Then you know why I'm doing this?" I grab his throat and start squeezing. "You finally recognize me?"

He gurgles, face purple like a bruise. "No."

The murder starts in my shoulders, surges down my arms and sizzles into the clamp around his neck. This is it, the grand reveal that I told you was coming since all the way back when.

"Shut up!" I let out the roar that's been building for more lifetimes than I'd care to count, shouting all the gathered voices into silence and demanding their witness. "Shut up and let me tell you!"

Let me, just. Just.

But I got nothing. No matter how deep I thrust into the chowder and wet toilet paper of these coagulated memories, pawing through the gabble and the jive, that part that was only mine just sinks further out of reach. A silver coin spinning into a stagnant fountain. A teardrop hitting the vanishing point on the horizon.

Everyone, living and otherwise, stares at me as I come up snake eyes. We all look down together, into this Friday's hands, where the Truck has already quietly expired without any fanfare or ado. Just passed on into the night, leaving this broken and soiled thing behind.

The crowd around the Pit begins to boo. The crowd inside joins them.

MISE EN ABYME

AFTER A YEAR OF MARRIAGE, I told my wife that I was going to write this story and call it "Mise en Abyme," which means "Placed into Abyss." Of course, if she'd told me not to, I wouldn't have, because I would do, or not do, anything for her. But she only said that there wasn't a need, that what has happened has happened and what will come will come.

We had been discussing, in a general sense, the problem of having children, when she told me that when she was a little girl, she would sometimes wake to find the outline of an old woman sitting on the corner of her bed. Neither her mother nor father believed her, but through half-open eyes she could see the pale skin and hair. She felt the mattress move under the woman's weight. In her room, a mirror stood beside the closet and another hung on the wall, and my wife very clearly remembered how the visitor's reflection, and the reflection of her reflection, curved away into a seemingly infinite bow.

The visitor spoke in just a whisper, so soft and so low that she almost couldn't hear it above the sound of the blood running its circuit through her ears. But it was always the same story, and after enough repetitions it carved deep grooves in the layers of her memory.

There's no stopping it now, of course, and we'll never be heroes, but there's more to it than that. This is still a love story.

───── ∾ ─────

By the time of the Great Return, Heira has worked for the Commitment's state-run television news organization for almost twenty-three years. Although listed merely as an "editor," and with only a single assigned responsibility, the level of respect accorded to her far exceeds that which could be expected merely from her relationship with the Overseer. Although unrecognized by the public, the deference paid to her by everyone from the Commitment's rank and file guards at traffic checkpoints and the station doors to the wives and husbands of top-ranking officials hovers between obsequious and religious. Chalmers, the oldest of the television station's guards and a veteran of the wars, sometimes even bows to her. It's an unnecessary and extravagant gesture, but some ripple of acknowledgment follows in her wake as she enters each afternoon to prepare for the nightly broadcast.

Every night, that is, until the beginning of the Great Return. That night, for the first time in over a decade, Chalmers stops Heira to check her identification. Entering the open room of the broadcast set, too, she's greeted by the backs of a crowd. Gathered like they were going to the gallows or arrayed for the firing squad, the newsroom's crew stands before the bank of monitors. They gasp and gape in silence, a row of tombstones undulating in the siren strobe of the screens.

"It's a rogue transmission," Nelson, her producer, whispers as Heira joins the ranks.

"Do you think"—the anchor, Carol Denish, takes up the satellite of rumor—"I mean, it's got to be an error, right?"

On the screen, Heira recognizes last night's regularly broadcast Corrective Executions. Once again Heira watches the old man led across the outdoor stage by soldiers in the Watch's black uniform. She watches the young girl follow, prodded by a rifle butt, and then the one-armed man with the shock of red hair. This was her work from last night, of course.

Or rather, it's not her work. Because, as the camera pans around from behind the imminent Corrections, Heira sees the difference. She sees their eyes.

The eyes that she had so painstakingly removed.

As the bullets punctuate their simple ellipses across the bodies and faces, the crowd before Heira hisses as the life drains from the eyes, the agony and the snuff of the spark unmasked. Heira, of course, has seen this—indeed, she is the one who must—but to the others this is new. The sterility and acceptability of the Corrective Executions, accomplished through Heira's work of minimalist censorship—the application of a flat black bar across the eyes of the Corrections—has been undone and the assembled crowd, too, appears undone.

It takes Heira a moment to realize that Nelson and several of the others are openly weeping.

The screen flickers, goes dark, wakes again. It blinks out the 5-4-3-2 of the intro reel and starts the loop again, camera beginning behind the old man, the young girl, the one-armed man. There is the wet sound and sudden smell of vomit.

She turns and finds that behind her, a camera is rolling. The steady red eye of the recording light glares without blinking, watching the people watching the screen. Footage for tonight, she thinks.

She's about to leave for the editing bay to begin redacting tonight's footage of today's Corrective Executions when it happens.

"That's enough," Nelson yells, as the regurgitated execution ends again and begins again for the third time since Heira has arrived. "Cut the feed." And somewhere beyond them, in the control room at the end of the producer's radio signal, a switch is flipped. The renegade naked feed is cut, swapped for the image from the camera recording the newsroom's reaction.

And in the monitors at the front, the new picture is within a picture within another. An infinite visual recursion of backs of heads staring into a screen showing the backs of heads staring into a screen, and so on at a slight angle, so that each iteration magnifies the bend until it seems to twist away into the dark recess of the television.

To Heira this new vision is the true gateway to abomination. This infinite stretching, twisting tunnel into an abyss within the screen. It stirs a memory within her. A voice. A repetition.

Then the monitors are cut and everything goes flat and black.

GORDON B. WHITE

Rumors swirl like ticker tape through the newsroom and in the gurgle of whispers in the rest of the Capitol District. Everyone has seen it. Everyone agrees on what it is. No one knows why or how, but theories range from wild to outlandish:

A political activist group with moles inside the state-run agencies, releasing unexpurgated footage of the nightly executions to foment rebellion.

A freak echo of the transmission signals, bouncing off of satellites and space debris in an ablation cascade of radio waves, the masking properties of the original stripped in the relay and returned to Earth without the necessary protections.

The blind ghosts of the bitter dead.

The old God and Its wrath.

That night, as she lies in bed next to the District's Overseer after a night of talking around the topic, Heira dreams of sitting in the editing bay and placing digital shrouds over the eyes of the old man, the young girl, the one-armed man. Then, feeling the oppressive weight of observation, she turns to find the pressing crowd behind her, gathered as if to watch a spider in a terrarium. There are Nelson and Carol, then the techs from Control, then the cameramen, but beyond them, where the peripheral lights dim, are people she doesn't recognize. Or that she does recognize, but whose names she never knew.

At the edge, a tiny figure scuttles into the tunnels between the observers' legs. The gargle of grey static emanates from the crowd, the susurration of fingers pushing through sand.

On her screen, the Corrective footage has vanished, replaced by the back of her own straw-colored head gazing into the monitor, its screen a picture of a woman gazing into a monitor with an image of a woman gazing into a monitor. The details at the finest level are too small to see, but at the center is a black pinprick, a single pixel—perhaps—that stands out like a dark star. As she leans in, the picture wavers. All of the lines rise, but as of yet do not converge. The hole at the center winks at her and calls her name.

<hr />

MISE EN ABYME

"This is, of course, a formality," the inspector begins, pressing a red button on the machine that squats in the middle of the table. A recording light blinks on, and there's a brief squall of feedback until the woman adjusts the dial. "But please, tell me about your work."

For so long Heira has been above reproach that the interview—not interrogation, not for her, never—by one of the Commitment's officers is a novelty. A secondhand tale told by others, but now Heira is in this barren room, staring into her reflection in the two-way mirror behind the inspector, living out a story within her story.

Heira tells the woman in the green uniform—or, rather, confirms, since the Commitment knows almost everything—most of her story. How she worked for a television station before the wars and the Shift. How afterwards, when the Commitment and the Districts were devised, she was already living in what became the Capitol. Heira waves away the years, as if they bullet out a plot to which everyone knows the ending. She was assigned the role of editor. She makes the nightly Corrective Executions safe for mandatory public consumption by removing the eyes. No, Heira doesn't have anything to do with the data afterwards. No, she doesn't know how the unredacted images were released.

"I mean no impudence," the inspector says, her blue eyes flashing, "but did your appointment have anything to do with the Overseer?"

"Almost everything has to do with the Overseer," Heira answers. "You'd have to ask him," she adds, knowing that the inspector won't.

The inspector ends the recording and signals to unseen compatriots behind the two-way mirror. As they both stand up and shake hands, however, in that moment before the door unlocks from the outside, the inspector leans in close. Her voice cracks slightly on inflection, worry wriggling through.

"How do you do it?"

It's the one thing that everybody wants to ask, although few ever do. How can Heira be the one to look into the eyes of the dead and take them away? How is it that while the public can only watch the Corrective Executions every night without flinching so long as the eyes are covered, Heira can stare into each window of the soul as it closes on their behalf? How does this one person, any person, manage to eat the sins of the Commitment every night?

Refracted within it is, *Why?*

"I've always known my calling," Heira answers, squeezing the inspector's hand. "What will come will come."

Although Heira is free of any suspicion, new protocols are still put in place. An armed guard delivers a thumb drive to Heira in a sealed manila envelope, then she is locked alone in the editing bay to upload it on a dedicated laptop with no external plugs and the wireless connectivity removed with pliers.

Heira reviews the footage—a woman with iron-grey hair who marches unbowed to the stage and receives a bullet to the temple. Her eyes are great and watery, but not weak.

A bald man, heavy with the weight of unhealthy habits and, from his gait, regrets. His hazel eyes twitch back and forth, as if looking for a way out, before the soldiers' guns make quick work of him.

Two children, a boy and a girl, as unlike each other as night and day. Except, however, for the shape of their brows and the slope of their lids. Little holes bloom in their chests as the force drives them back into the drop cloth on the stage.

Who else would notice, she wonders, as she sets about cutting out the eyes with this clean and isolated machine. She crops them, checks them, runs the new program, which doesn't just overlay the bars but punches them out of the digital data. She doesn't know how it works, but Raymond from Control said that all the ones and zeroes—the binary blink of data—are purged. Nothing to trace back, nothing to undo. Impervious to the piracy.

Heira breaks the factory seal on a clean thumb drive and downloads the edited footage. She hands it off to the guard, who takes the precaution of smashing the original drive with the original eyes into a dozen pieces that he grinds under his boot heel, leaving the wreckage in a heap on the floor.

MISE EN ABYME

The Corrective Executions air at 6 pm, as usual. By 7 pm, the uncensored footage is being looped on the pirate channel. By 7:01 pm, the Overseer is on the phone screaming at the station manager, and by 7:14 pm, the riot officers are in the street quelling dissent with batons and fire hoses.

Rubber bullets by 8:20 pm, live fire by 9.

Until the night shift finishes at 3 am and an armed escort takes her home, Heira sits at her desk, pointing a web camera at her monitor, swinging the Droste effect tunnel of the picture in a picture across the screen, trying to find the end point. Through a tiny hole that opens and closes, she hears a voice so low that it's almost a whisper.

The next day, the armed guard brings the data stick in and as soon as it's uploaded, Heira pulls it from the new triple-locked laptop and smashes the stick into two dozen pieces on the top of her desk.

The armed guard blanches, but doesn't stop her, as Heira sweeps the shards into her palm, then into her mouth. She swallows. The pieces cut going in, and she knows they'll cut going out, but that's for tomorrow. Feeling the sick pulse in her stomach, she holds it down while she edits the day's footage. Two women, green eyes. A man, dark brown.

At 6 pm, the Corrective Executions air. By 6:37 pm, the unaltered footage is on the rogue transmission. The Overseer doesn't call the station because the district is already under curfew and everyone out past the broadcast—with the exception of Heira and other authorized Commitment personnel with police escort—is executed under Operating Order 7.B(4).

This is the new standard procedure as the situation worsens over the coming days.

Heira wakes up and crawls out of bed, over to the television set on the dresser. She turns it on and the blue image flickers and bows, the screen itself flexing like the surface of a bubble before it settles. The image is, as she knew it would be, a shot from behind of her watching the screen, on which she is watching herself watching herself in ever-smaller iterations. She raises one hand, and the wave of Heiras ripples as they follow suit. Perfectly aligned in the center of the screen is a dark hole, the screen on the screen on the screen, ad infinitum.

Static kisses the fingertip she places on the dot, and there's a slight resistance as she wiggles it, working her finger into the minuscule hole in the membrane of the screen. It's tight, but gives way with enough pressure.

She watches as the rows upon rows of Heiras on the screens do the same, their fingers and arms aligning into a single flesh-colored shaft. Up to her knuckle already in the vortex of the screens within the screen, she works another finger in beside it. Inside it is smooth, and it bends and gives. Beneath her fingertips, the canal of regressive images curls away from her, but she pushes harder. Her remaining fingers enter, then her thumb. Her forearm. The series of images stretches to accommodate her further and further as she turns to the side, thrusting shoulder-deep into the hole in the center of the centers of the pictures. From the corner of her right eye against the screen, she can see the left side shown in the infinitely smaller repetitions. The look on the Heiras' faces surprises her, their lip-bitten determination and furrowed concentration.

Then she twists and, with some effort, forces her head into the puckering hole, wiggling her other arm in beside it. There is nothing to see, a complete absence of light, but still she wriggles in deeper, feeling her way through the crevices as she kicks in fully, inching deeper and deeper. Waves of contractions in the muscular walls press her into herself and pull her deeper inside.

Still, Heira forces her way.

After what may be hours or centuries or seconds, there is a faint pinhole of illumination. She pushes onward, arms extended, until her fingers pop free, protruding out into a warm and humid port of air. She pulls and pulls, sliding arms- and head-first out into a vast space and tumbling down the slick walls to the moist floor in the sweltering darkness. Above her, dim and blinking stars hang like bats from the roof of the abyss.

MISE EN ABYME

Heira cannot say what it is that she sees, but the very walls and floors of the cavern seem alive. In the days after, her imagination drafts and re-drafts the horror: A great blind Worm rolling in the swollen womb beneath the center of human consciousness. A Mole God in its lair, tunneling out into the realms of possibility, waiting to emerge into the light and devour the sun. A limbless Crone, lost in the abscesses between spaces and times and grown impossibly huge and pale and boneless, thatches of straw-colored hair above empty eye-pits that glisten red as rare meat. But these terrible things pale beside the Great Voice that begins to speak.

"If I were to choose an apostle," the Great Voice speaks, its words rolling through the dark organ of its lair, "I would choose you. You are the witness and do not flinch. Others have lost their sense, but you are immune, whether by nature or by practice. Yes, if there was one, it would be you, it has always been you.

"But I have no need for conversion, and I have no need for further witnesses. You have served well, but what more could you offer me out there?"

As her eyes grow accustomed to the faint glow of the corpulent stars and the pinched illumination from the edges of other tunnels, Heira can make out movements around her. Pale and spindle-boned, woman-shaped things crawl like tapeworms from other tunnels and skitter around the edges of her sight before burrowing headfirst into new pathways. High above them, the luminescent globes flicker and blink their dim light. The air smells raw and internal, the scent of a wound that will never heal and never fester.

Through the closer tunnels, the gouges in the gargantuan pustule's lining, Heira catches flashes of other places and other times. A reflection of herself in her own eyes in the two-way mirror of the interview room, just over the fearful inspector's shoulder. The glass picture frame in a bedroom, glaring over two post-coital bodies in the bed below to stare into the glossy, empty reflection of a dead television.

A silhouette sitting at the foot of a bed, whispering to a little girl pretending to be asleep. The phalanx of shadows between the mirror on the wall and the mirror by the closet bows on and on, out of her sight, looping on into another infinity. Maybe even back into this chamber.

Reeling in the dampness, constricted in the belly of the abyss, Heira begins to hyperventilate. As if sensing her agitation, the ground roils and trembles; contractions squeeze and heave. The pale figures on the periphery scatter like maggots back into the meat and the lights above her shudder and then begin to fall.

And then Heira realizes they are not lights. They are eyes. Angry, sad, confused, flickering in a panoply of colors, they swarm around her, propelled by their fluttering lids like moths' wings. Their wet, heavy blinking is the sound of hundreds and thousands of mouths, and their butterfly kisses are thick and viscous, sopping with fur-like lashes. As they bite, rubbing their lids against her skin to pull and grasp, she screams. The cavern spasms, forcing her into one of the open furrows, expelling her from the Great Voice's audience with pulsations while the disembodied eyes nip at her bare soles. As the skin of the walls closes around her mouth, Heira cannot move, cannot breathe, and can no longer scream.

Darkness on all sides, in all aspects.

Then it starts again.

"Someone at the end of the tunnel," the Great Voice says, "is writing your story. Someone is always telling it again and again.

"What is coming is the Terrible Narration, the final story in the *mise en abyme*. The last chapter is the one in the middle, the final moment that returns not to the beginning but to the center.

"Worms and moles do not need eyes, yet here they are, alongside a god with nothing to touch and no perfect future. One grown fat and strong on all your commitment and willing sacrifice, but still demanding more and more.

MISE EN ABYME

"And yet, in the darkness, the eyes are blinking and the reflections off their tears are being translated into a story called 'Placed in Abyss,' where you carry on in divine repetition.

"They are twinkling in the earth like shards of mica. They are flickering like stars. Somewhere, sometime, the story of your success, which is your failure, which is the place in the abyss, is being written and re-written.

"You need only to connect it."

Burrowing through the layers of blankets like a nightcrawler escaping from flooded tunnels, Heira wakes, gasping in the night air. Beside her, the Overseer sleeps, sheets encasing his twitching legs like a tail. The orange light of the streetlamp reticulates them both through the blinds' slatted shadows.

Heira knows, then, the truth of the endless passage and the hole at the center of the picture-in-a-picture. It isn't only that it's a grave worm's tunnel, opening up into the Great Voice's living catacomb. It is also a birth canal, a great heaving cervix with the Great Voice within preparing to emerge, slurping out like a giant tongue and vomiting its vanguard of dead men's eyes back into the world.

Eyes that glisten like eggs, flapping on heavy-lidded wings.

The Corrective Executions and their broadcasts, of course, continue. The Overseer takes to the radio to warn that insubordination and curfew violations have been declared capital crimes. Religious and civil leaders are subject to particular scrutiny, and dealt with quickly by the Commitment.

Protestors swarm the street en masse, eyes covered by opaque visors or heavy black blindfolds that mimic the bars that Heira places over the eyes of the continued Corrective Executions. These dissidents are themselves executed on the sidewalks and in the alleys by impromptu groups of police and vigilantes, their bodies left for the municipal services or the rats to sort out.

Within the hour of any mass shooting, however, footage appears on the pirate waves. Even when officers swear that protestors wore the visors, even where the remnants of the corpses' faces are still held together only by black bands, the footage shows their eyes.

They flicker, then are pinched like candle wicks.

"If there is a window to the soul," the Overseer asks Heira as they lie in bed, still damp from their exertion, "where do you think it is?" He kisses her closed eyes, her lips, all the while his hands roaming down across her naked belly, into her lap.

He doesn't taste like murder, she thinks. Does he even understand what he's doing?

Around them the room is mad with reflections. In the picture frames, the mirrors, the window backed by the darkness outside, the empty screen of the television that Heira no longer allows him to turn on. In all of these positions, Heira and the Overseer are reflected—two layers, three, four, five, on into the illusion of forever. However, they are always incomplete, always that one degree off that spins the multitude of regressions into a slow curve away from the truly infinite.

She pulls his hands away and opens her eyes. She can see her reflection in his deep blue gaze, her face placed in the middle of the chasm of his pupil. Maybe, she thinks, something is moving in the distance.

If only she could find her way back.

The Overseer has come to the news station for an emergency broadcast. Their staff diminished though desertion and violence, the remainder has shrunk well past "skeleton crew," and now the station is haunted by the rumor of a ghost of a news team. Still, they stand on ceremony for the Overseer and his military escort, although the typical pomp has been replaced by an air reminiscent of the recent funerals of heads of the Commitment.

"Sir, your wife is here," the guard says, opening the door to the green room for Heira.

"Are you ready?" Heira asks, crossing to where the Overseer readies himself before the mirror.

"Of course," the Overseer smiles. He leans, and she closes her eyes to be kissed on the lids. "I've always loved you."

"I never wanted this," she says. "But I've always known, you know?"

Of course he knows. There are no secrets between them, and there never have been. He puts a finger to her lips.

"It's all right," the Overseer says. "What has happened has happened."

She nods. "And what will come will come."

"Then I'll see you again."

~~~

As the Overseer enters the stage, Heira takes her place behind the camera. These days, even the Overseer's wife and the editor of the Commitment takes a laboring oar.

As the producer checks the Overseer's microphone, he whispers to his superior.

"Heira once told me that before the Shift, you wrote a book or a novel or something. Something about"—he looks over his shoulder at the empty studio—"this?"

The Overseer nods. "A story, yes, called 'Mise en Abyme.'"

"How did it end?" There is a glimmer in his eyes that could have been hope, if it didn't suspect the truth.

But the Overseer grips the producer's shoulder, squeezes it once, then turns to walk to his mark in front of the large and empty monitor. Through his tears, the producer counts down the 5-4-3-2, and they are on the air.

~~~

"Fellow subjects of the Commitment," the Overseer begins, the giant monitor behind him displaying live footage of the rioters just outside the station and the ragged line of soldiers holding them at bay.

"I know that you have heard rumors and misinformation. That the Commitment has lost control. That our believers have betrayed us, that our technology has failed. That the God we left behind has come back to deal with us.

"This is foolish."

Beyond the station's doors, the roar of the wave of the crowd surges and, on the monitor, it crashes against the final bulwark of the Commitment, beginning to break through the beleaguered remnant.

"For indeed, we are on the cusp of a great new beginning. You ask, why then do we not stop the Corrective Executions? Why do we not stop broadcasting them? Because, my fellows, there are purposes and meanings to your sacrifices that even you do not know. Not yet.

"But I understand what you want. You want to again understand your place in existence. You want assurance that the terror of history, the stream that runs from the past ever onward to the abyssal ocean of infinity, can change course. That there is a way out.

"Well, your sacrifices have not been in vain. Your suffering has proven worthy. If you doubt the Commitment, if you think that it has become too weak and too human in its petty vanities and desires, then I offer you a cleansing. Today, and forever, is the Re-Commitment.

"Gather your family around the television. Turn on every screen. Watch closely."

Someone screams in the halls, and the locked doors of the studio shudder in their chains and groan on their hinges. Heira pushes a button, and the screen behind the Overseer flips over to her camera's feed. A receding line of Overseers, each more indistinct than the last, stretches off into the distance. So many versions of her husband, each dedicated entirely to her and the Grand Return she's been heralding since she was only a girl. He steps aside now, lets the void of the empty screen show itself upon itself again and again and again and again.

It curves slightly, but Heira pans the camera over, searching for the proper alignment. At the far end of the tunnel, almost microscopic, the darkness blinks.

MISE EN ABYME

She prepares herself for the flood of eyes that will precede the Great Voice made flesh. For the Great Voice itself in all its splendor.

For the gaping hole she will crawl back into to start the cycle again.

———————

I asked Heira if she wanted to read "Mise en Abyme," to see if I've missed any details or taken any liberties, but she declined. She knows it well enough to tell by heart.

"Don't judge me too harshly," she said. "I mean, if I have to leave you, afterwards."

But I took her hand, my sweet wife, for whom I would do anything. I whispered back the words that we will one day say again.

"What has happened will come."

"And what will come has happened."

"Then I'll see you again."

Beyond us, in the darkness, the Great Voice is calling. The Worm is turning.

EIGHT AFFIRMATIONS FOR THE REVOLTING BODY, CONFISCATED FROM THE PRISONERS OF BUNK 17

8. "My body cannot be owned. It is not my possession; rather, my body is myself. As I include my body into my sense of self, empathy for its story is the only thing left to feel."

LOW, BOOMING THUNDER SEEPS UP along the distant night sky as Maria staggers across the prison yard from the Geesler's administrative cabin back towards Bunk 17. The other bunkhouses around the camp are quiet and dark, even the ones that still have occupants behind their shuttered windows. The empty watchtowers around the barbed wire fences are blinded eyestalks on the perimeter. Again, Maria hopes that the end is coming soon, that human troops will reach the camp while there are still prisoners left to save.

When Maria enters, alone, the nineteen remaining women of Bunk 17 rise and descend from their tiered beds to converge on her. In the dim light through the grimy panes, she can see that, contrary to regulations, many of the prisoners are still dressed. For a moment, habit tells her to yell at them, but she knows that stripped of her role as the prisoner functionary and evicted from her separate quarters, she has no more protection from either their alien captors or from her gaunt former charges that now circle her like dogs.

"Where's Amanda?" Sonja demands. The other women mutter.

"The Geesler took her," Maria says.

"You're not in charge anymore," Dee says. Her upper lip is split, and the pink bud of her tongue flicks out to touch the raw gash. "Where is she?"

"The Geesler, you stupid cow," Maria says as she turns her back on Dee and lets her sackcloth jacket slide off her shoulders to the bare floor. A few of the prisoners stare at the fresh and gaping wound on Maria's arm, but they don't ask where it's from. "It—its Masters, whatever—have taken her, and if I don't give them one more body, they're going to eat all of you, too."

"You did this," Dee says, and grabs Maria's injured arm.

"Fuck all of you." Maria turns, swinging at Dee and catching her full in the face. Dee falls like a match into a powder keg, and the other women explode.

Their fists hit Maria in the stomach, crack her ribs, smash her breasts, and bruise her organs. Maria has no time to raise her defense before the blows crumple her to the floor and the others begin to kick and stomp.

Work boots and bare feet crush Maria's midsection and, as she curls up, her arms and legs and hips and head, as well. Dee watches as Sonja and Carly and Karsen and the other fifteen women crush Maria, pouring out the anger accreted over months and months of imprisonment in the Geesler's camp. All the labor, the starvation, the disappearances—Maria is the symptom they attack with the fury of every antibody against oppression.

"Fucking traitor," Carly screams as she digs her toes into Maria's dented side.

"Sadistic bitch," Karsen yells as she drives a heel into Maria's open mouth.

Dee cries as she, too, kicks and kicks and kicks.

The women break Maria's ribs and arms. Skull fractures roll out like lines on a tectonic map, the broken plates pushing into her brain. The women don't stop. They keep punching, kicking, spitting, and smashing with shoes and bits of wood until Maria stops moving.

The women stand around her broken body. Her eyes are half-open, but glossy like the bunk windows. Blood oozes from her myriad wounds across the unfinished wooden floors, dripping down through the uneven cracks. In the blue moonlight punctuated by distant bursts of red, it seems almost as if Maria is breathing in the shifting light. When the flashes stop, however, she is undeniably dead.

"They can't do this to us again," Karsen says, breathing heavily.

The nearest women grab Maria's body, wrapping fingers into her rough garments and around disjointed limbs. One woman reaches for Maria's head, but Dee pushes her away and picks up Maria's loose and rolling neck. She looks at the blackened lips, the cracked teeth and the uneven eyes. A tear falls from Dee's cheek onto Maria's.

"Throw her outside for the Geesler," Sonja says. She points to the ragged hole in Maria's arm—the one wound that the prisoners didn't cause. "If they want to eat someone, they can eat her."

"She's the last," Dee says. "No more."

"No more," the women agree.

The paltry procession throws Maria's body outside onto the ground. It flops over and lies in the mud, all broken angles in the darkness. From the shadows around its office, the Geesler snuffles, drawn by the scent of blood.

7. "First they ignore you. Then they laugh at you. Then they eat you. Make them sick."

In the lurid violets and carnations of the setting sun, Justine dragged Maria across the muddy yard to the Geesler's cabin. Maria, for all her anger, offered no resistance as Justine hauled her by the sleeve of her sackcloth jacket, muddy boots scrabbling, up the wooden steps to the Geesler's office. The metal bar and lock across the door gave beneath Justine's turn, and she shoved Maria inside.

The Geesler leaned against its office cabinet for dramatic effect. Maria didn't know what it looked like beneath the body it wore as a costume, or even how much of it was filled by the creature, but it had re-adjusted the corpse-skin around its frame to look almost human. The dim light from the Geesler's desk lamp concealed the seams that it had ripped that morning, but the cheeks still hung slack above the

Geesler's concealed throat sack. The yellow sclera and iris of its eyes clicking open and closed seemed intended to annoy her.

"Delgado," the Geesler said to Maria while waving Justine out. "Time's up."

"I'm not quitting," Maria said.

The Geesler swayed towards its desk, thrusting its hips out awkwardly, stomach pushing too far forward and arms akimbo. It took two steps, then suddenly careened forward, limp arms slapping the desk in mocking emphasis.

"You're fired." The true mouth beneath its skin mask pulled up at the corners in a smile. "Turn in your badge."

The Geesler reached over and dug a finger behind Maria's purple armband that designated her as Prisoner Functionary—one of the Geesler's conscripted servants in the camp. The band slid to the table beneath the Geesler's dead hand. Without its protection, a former functionary that returned to the bunkhouses was dead within two nights. At best.

"They'll kill me," Maria said.

"Probably," the Geesler said, restraining its smiling mouthparts so as not to re-burst the skin that it hid beneath. "But you're done."

"Why?"

"Are you seriously—" the Geesler sputtered. "Because you have a revolutionary element that you can't control. Because your prisoners are so scrawny that the other bunks call them the 'Skeleton Crew.' Because the Masters are—No. You're done."

"You can't take my position," Maria says.

"It's already gone," the Geesler said. The cabin door opened again, and Maria turned to see Amanda struggling against Justine's grip. When Amanda saw the Geesler for the first time up close, however, she froze. With the back of its hand, the Geesler slid the purple armband across the desk towards Amanda.

"You're the functionary now," the Geesler said. "You get to show the others who's boss."

Amanda stared at the armband, and Maria wondered if she would actually take it.

"Pick it up," the Geesler said, and Justine pushed Amanda

forward. Amanda, all thin shoulders and bony waist, was no match for Justine's well-fed bulk, but as she fell forward, Maria lunged for the band.

The Geesler shot forward and caught Maria by the hand. It jerked her towards its side of the desk, stretching her out across the papers on top.

Maria pulled against the Geesler, but it was too strong. With one clammy hand wrapped around her wrist, the Geesler slowly pushed up the sleeve of Maria's jacket. Looking past Maria towards Amanda, it gently lowered its maw of needle teeth and, for a second, moist breath and spittle flecked the soft underside of Maria's arm.

Then the Geesler bit down. Sharp teeth dug in and then it pulled back, ripping out a chunk as Maria screamed. Amanda screamed, too, and even Justine gasped.

The Geesler let go and leaned back, a string of blood and saliva oozing from its slack lips. It gurgled, almost purring as it swallowed.

"Goddam it," the Geesler said, wiping its mouth with the back of its hand and smearing the blood. "Why is everything with you such a mess?"

It sighed dramatically as Maria cradled her mangled arm.

"Now pick it up," the Geesler said, and Amanda, trembling, picked up the purple armband. "Good. Now take her to her cabin," it said, flailing its hand towards Amanda. Justine dragged her out of the room, still stunned.

"You," the Geesler said to Maria. "Back to the bunk."

Her skin waxy with the sweat of shock, Maria leaned across the desk. "How'd I taste?" she asked.

"Bitter," the Geesler said.

Maria rose to leave, the trails of blood still running from her ragged wound.

"Oh," the Geesler said, flopping its hand over in a play of nonchalance. "And to show you I'm serious, I want one more outside, for us, in the next ten minutes. Or I'll fucking burn your bunk down and eat them all myself."

6. "All oppression creates a state of war. One writes fables in periods of oppression."

The watery soup that Sonja had prepared from Bunk 17's meager dinner rations smelled delicious as Maria approached the mess tent. Low and distant booms of something like thunder trembled in the evening air, and on the edge of the gloaming Maria could almost see the red glow of fires, or perhaps even rockets. The war was coming closer, she told herself. Some of them might make it after all.

When she saw the gaunt line, Maria knew that she shouldn't keep the women from eating tonight, too. Although some women had embraced the asceticism counseled in the subversive slogans, the stress fractures were already showing up in everyone's eyes and splitting into their voices. There was a savage hunger in the way all the women stared at her when she entered the tent. Maria felt their collective hatred as the figurehead of their torment.

Maria waited until about half of the twenty women had gone through the line—the thinnest and weakest, bless the others—until Amanda and Dee were beside each other, waiting for their portion of soup and bread. She watched as Sonja dipped the ladle deep, stirring up a few lonely beans from the bottom of the pot, which she skimmed into Amanda's bowl. Dee touched Amanda on the elbow and smiled. Maria had become adept at noticing these small gestures of solidarity.

Dee turned and saw Maria watching them. The look in Dee's eyes was almost one that Maria recognized from the days they had spent together before she was a functionary. It wasn't affection, though, but a sad kind of sympathy.

"Stop there," Maria said. Everyone in the mess froze. The only sound was the soup bubbling. "Are you passing messages?"

Dee's eyes flickered from confusion to hurt to anger, then stuck there. "How can you ask me that?"

Maria grabbed Dee and pushed her down, bending her over the table. Digging her elbow into Dee's spine, Maria pinned her in place, then shoved a hand up under Dee's shirt. She pulled out a wadded-up slip of paper. "What is this?"

"I don't know." Dee struggled under Maria's weight.

Maria unfolded the paper with one hand and read it out: "*All oppression creates a state of war.* What the fuck is this?" She threw it at the feet of the assembling crowd.

"You planted it," Dee said.

"You liar." Maria pulled Dee up and then shoved her back. Dee's leg tangled with a table's leg, and she twisted to fall face-first to the ground.

Someone grabbed Maria's arm. Amanda. Maria shook her off and stepped back in case anyone planned to take a swing. Dee stood, her lip split and bleeding down her chin.

Maria pointed to Amanda, then the soup. "Pour it out."

"No." There was a hard look in Amanda's eyes. "You can't have it."

"Pour it the fuck out," Maria said. "Or I'll feed you to the Geesler myself before the war ends."

"Stop saying that," Dee screamed.

The crowd was rumbling, and Maria spun around to see the ranks closing around her. She grabbed the closest bowl from the table and hurled it across the tent, striking the big pot on the burner. The hot liquid splashed up and hung for a moment in the air before it fell to the ground. Sonja hopped backwards as boiling droplets glittered and nipped at her patches of bare skin.

"Losing control?" Justine said, seemingly appearing from thin air in the entrance to the mess.

"I'm in charge," Maria said. She looked at the hungry circle of women around her. "Everything is going according to plan."

"Geesler wants you," Justine said. She gestured for Maria to follow.

"I won't tell you all again," Maria said to the crowd as she left the tent. "If it comes down to you—any of you, all of you—or me, someone is going to die."

5. "Life doesn't start 10 pounds from now, it's already started. I make the choice to include myself in it."

If they were going to survive, there could be no weak links, and Amanda was the weakest one; Maria could tell. She reminded Maria of plenty of good women from the world before the Geesler and its kind arrived, before the war began and they started rounding people up. For now, though, while Amanda sat on the periphery of the other women's conversations as they waited to enter the shower tent before returning for dinner, Maria reminded herself that the best of them were already gone.

Maria waited until Dee went into the shower, her hands torn and bleeding but refusing to cry; then she stalked across the yard. Carly and Karsen were talking next to Amanda, but fell silent as Maria approached, and it was only too late that their silence registered with Amanda. She was gnawing on her lip, and when she raised her head and opened her mouth in stunned surprise, Maria couldn't help but stare at the glistening pink corner of chewed-over flesh. She almost felt sorry for her.

"Up," Maria said. Amanda was only halfway to her feet before Maria was in her face. "What do you know about the subversive messages?"

Amanda stuttered, but Maria pinned her with a finger in the chest. Amanda looked from face to face across the line like a searchlight.

"Look at me," Maria said. "They aren't going to help you."

"I, I don't—"

"You're sitting here, listening to these two rattle on about resistance, and you're silent. Is that because you know who's behind it?"

"I wasn't even talking to them," Amanda said.

"Or are you gathering info for the Geesler?"

Carly laughed. "Resistance is vain."

Maria shut her up with one glare, then turned back to Amanda. "You're going to break, and the only question is which way," she said. "Stop looking around! Nobody here is going to help you."

Amanda was silent. The circle of women pressing in around them was silent. The late afternoon's cold air was still and for a second everything was frozen, just waiting for one of them to crack.

EIGHT AFFIRMATIONS

"You loser," Maria finally snapped. "You're too weak. Why don't you just kill yourself and let the Geesler eat you?"

"I don't want to die," Amanda said.

"That doesn't make you special."

"Leave her alone," Sonja said, and stepped forward. A few other brave souls seemed ready to follow.

Events were escalating, but Maria was ready, so she grabbed a fistful of Sonja's still-wet hair and with a great wrench pulled her aside. The shriek that pierced the air stopped everyone. Maria shoved Sonja into a gaggle of the other women who bent under the weight, but kept her from falling back into the muck.

"If it's you or me," Maria spit at the group, "it's going to be me."

The crowd was silent.

"Since everybody seems to love you," Maria said, and pointed to Amanda, "you're in charge. Don't turn your back on them."

Maria entered the shower tent alone, stripped, and stood beneath the freezing trickle of water. She tried to let her mind go as the icy rivulets ran across her body, but all she could think about was how before the war her skin had been soft and she'd had curves. Now she was hard lines and her ribs protruded like the bars of a cage beneath her skin. She was always cold.

Outside, the whispers of the women were low and hushed, an ominous rumble in the distance. Maria rinsed the clots of mud that crusted in the tangle of her hair. She wondered if the others were turning on Amanda or coming to her side. If any other functionary saw the women unattended, they would report Maria for creating dangerous and possibly subversive situations. For now, though, she didn't care, because beyond the shower tent's stale air laden with mildewed canvas and the stink of human bodies, Maria could almost smell the pine trees outside the camp. In the spring, there might even be the scent of wildflowers from just beyond the barbed wire. She hoped that she would be there to see their pink blossoms blowing in the wind.

Maria finished. She dried and dressed again in her single pair of clothes, stiff with dirt. She adjusted her purple armband and exited the tent to find the women facing her in a line, as silent as the mountains. Amanda stood directly in front. She still bit that red and worried patch of skin in the corner of her lip, but there was something stronger in her eyes. Amanda probably wouldn't break.

"Back in the truck," Maria said. The long strands of her hair were beginning to freeze.

4. "Resistance is vain; it only leads to struggle while inviting grief and sorrow. Vanity, however, shapes our bodies to resist."

Maria leaned against the transport truck that had brought the prisoners in her charge to the camp's edge. They were digging another useless ditch along the razor wire for use as defense or graves or latrines or in preparation for some other event that would hopefully never come. As her women's shovels cut through the slate-colored muck, emptying a furrow in the earth that the watery sediment slipped back in to refill, Maria smoked a cigarette from her functionary's rations. She exhaled, the smoke from her mouth obscuring the women behind it, transfiguring them into long-legged herons bobbing in a marsh, the necks of their shovels dipping up and down. Then the knife's edge of the wind rose again and cut away the haze, exposing the gristly women toiling before her. Maria wiped her nose as the drips at her nostrils froze despite the mid-morning sun's cold rays.

The women in the ditch stared at Maria as they worked. She felt the hate coming off of them. At the beginning of the shift, Maria had been there when Carly found the message at the shovel bin that read, "*Resistance is vain,*" et cetera, and so she'd taken their work gloves as punishment. These messages had been appearing more and more lately, a mix of patronizing and empowering nonsense that before the war might have appeared on affirmation websites, but now had become a strange call to arms and legs and torsos in the camp. The Geesler wanted them stamped out, lest the hungry unrest of Bunk 17 spread to other parts of the camp.

The women in Bunk 17 were all at least ten pounds lighter than they would have been under the other functionaries. At least, however, there were also still twenty women in Bunk 17, and no one had been "transferred" from under Maria's watch in weeks. Other functionaries like Justine said that it was because the Geesler and its Masters needed healthier labor, but Maria didn't believe that. She worked her women until they were lean and hard and hateful. Maria's prisoners weren't worth the trouble while there were still softer, more pliant prisoners in the other bunks.

As Maria watched, Dee nodded to a group of women standing around her, then pulled herself out of the trench. Covered in mud and shovel in hand, Dee walked towards Maria like a grey ghost against the brilliant green forests and the distant blue mountains just outside their patch of prison. Maria's stomach fluttered. She should have told Dee to turn back immediately and return to the detail. She couldn't afford to project any air of weakness or lingering favoritism.

"Can I talk to you?" Dee said, close and quiet enough that the others wouldn't hear, even though they were watching.

"No. Back on detail."

"Why not?" Dee held out her shovel as she leaned over to tug at her boot. Even before Maria realized it, the old habits of affection had taken it from Dee's hand. "We need to talk," Dee said, straightening, "about how the others feel."

"We don't," Maria said.

"Most of them are suffering."

"Most?"

"Some of them have been listening to those messages. They're starving themselves. They think they're resisting."

Maria took a deep breath. "Well?"

"The others are unhappy and—"

Maria slapped the shovel back into Dee's hand, smacking it against her callused palm.

"They're not going to get any happiness here," Maria said.

"If not happiness, then compassion."

"You don't need compassion. You need a purpose."

"And that purpose is work?"

Maria bit her lip. "It can be."

"The women in the other bunks are in better shape," Dee said. "They're healthier."

"They're weaker."

"They work inside and don't get punished with labor details like we do."

"So?"

"Their functionaries are kinder." Dee looked into Maria's eyes. "You've become pointlessly cruel."

Maria sniffed. "There's a point."

"What point?"

"You have to be stronger than the others, and whether you do it because of me or in spite of me, it doesn't matter."

"Why, though? Why do you think we have to do this?"

Maria wanted to grab Dee and shake her, but she gritted her teeth instead. "Because otherwise they'll kill you and they'll eat you."

"That's not true," Dee said.

"Of course it's true," Maria said. "You see how there are fewer and fewer people in the other bunks."

"That's release programs," Dee said. "You knew that before, but the pressure is getting to you."

"It's not," Maria says.

"It's not the Geesler killing people."

"Of course it is." Maria looked her in the eye. "And it's getting worse. The end of the war is coming, and the Geesler and its Masters are going to eat us all if they can."

"You can't keep saying that," Dee said.

"That they'll eat us?"

"That the end of the war is getting closer."

Maria became aware of her heart pounding and the ragged breaths whistling through her nose. She smelled the reek of the dirt and sweat, but above that, something cold and clean was blowing in through the links of the fence—something bright from the world beyond their walls.

"It's true," Maria said.

"It's not," Dee said. "We don't know how long it's going to be, but we need to survive and we need your help. You've convinced yourself about things that aren't true, and so you don't let us eat. You work us too hard. We won't last."

"If you don't like it," Maria said, "when they make you functionary, you can do it differently."

"I couldn't do it at all," Dee said.

"I know," Maria said. "That's why I have to."

"You don't have to be so tough. You could try to be kind."

Maria snapped: "If I'm kind, then you're weak. I have to— Never mind."

"Tell me," Dee said. "Please."

For a moment Maria might have, but then she saw the other women in the trench staring at them.

"Back on detail," Maria grunted, and she grabbed Dee's collar and dragged her back towards the lip of the hole, muddy boots scrabbling. She took the shovel from Dee's hands and threw it back into the trench, nearly hitting two other women.

"Dig until your hands bleed," Maria said, pointing back into the pit, "or no one gets to leave."

"I have tough hands," Dee said.

"Then you've got a lot of work to do."

3. "Food is not good or bad. It has no moral significance. I can choose to be good or bad, and it has nothing to do with the amount of calories or carbohydrates I eat. I choose not to be food."

There was always work to do and so, despite Maria's delay in the Geesler's office, the women from Bunk 17 were preparing breakfast in the mess tent when Maria entered. Maria made them take the earliest of meal shifts, so Sonja was already standing by the large pot of gruel she had prepared—every bunk was responsible for its own—and was ladling the first serving into Karsen's tin dish.

"Stop," Maria said, her voice cutting through the tent. "Step away."

With great reluctance, Karsen put her plate down and stepped back. Sonja hooked her ladle back around the lip of the pot. Maria tucked her thumbs behind her belt and sauntered to the front of the line. She looked closely at the edge of the counter, then reached underneath it and pulled out a folded slip of paper. She opened it, then read aloud:

"Food is not good or bad. It has no moral significance. I can choose to be good or bad, and it has nothing to do with the amount of calories or carbohydrates I eat. I choose not to be food."

She turned to the women. "Who wrote this?"

The twenty women of Bunk 17 all stared at Maria as she walked down the serving line. The first person was Karsen, her bowl already filled with the gruel. She clenched her bony knuckles at her side, thin arms trembling with the strain of not looking strained.

"Was it you?" Maria asked

"We all struggle," Karsen said. "That's just what being human is."

Maria slapped the bowl off of her tray and onto the floor. The liquid seeped into the ash-colored dirt.

"You?" Maria asked the next woman, Carly.

"I'm not good or bad," Carly sneered. "I didn't have anything to do with it."

Maria threw Carly's empty bowl on the floor. "Who else didn't have anything to do with it?"

All around her, the women stared with hollow eyes. The pot of gruel at Sonja's station bubbled away, its greasy liquid roiling, oblivious to the atmosphere around it.

"Then nobody eats," Maria said, and tipped the pot onto the floor. The women gasped as Maria dragged her boots through the slurry, mixing it into the grey mud and complete inedibility.

"So you're done?" someone asked. At the flap to the tent, the cook for Bunk 24—Functionary Justine's remaining prisoners—blocked the light with her wide hips and thick shoulders. The gnarled women of Bunk 17 turned and stared. The hunger in their eyes was palpable as they eyed the sack of provisions containing dried bacon and an extra tin of lard that hung across the woman's thigh.

"Bunk 17," Maria shouted, "get to the truck. Leaving in three."

The women of Bunk 17 slogged out into the mud of the prison

yard. They passed the first of the remaining twelve members of Bunk 24, already rising, their rested eyes and round stomachs making Maria's crew look skeletal by comparison.

2. "Just because someone looks perfect on the outside, doesn't mean they have a perfect life. We all struggle. That's just what being human is."

The grey mud sucked at Maria's boots as she walked across the yard towards Bunk 17. The scummy water sluiced into the treads of her steps, catching the first rays of sunlight and turning them to flame. Bunk 17 squatted among the other, mostly empty, structures. Its windows were dark, but Maria could see her women moving behind the grimy panes like fish in murky water. They knew Maria well enough that they would be ready to go when she arrived.

"Hey, Delgado." A voice cut across the yard and Maria turned to see Justine—the prisoner functionary from Bunk 24—leaning against the post at the Geesler's cabin office. Justine was heavy, weighing maybe half as much again as Maria, and she threw herself into each step as she approached.

"Geesler wants you," Justine said. She leaned in close and twisted her lips as if she was going to bite, but Maria held her gaze. "Well, get in there."

Maria left Justine and crossed towards the Geesler's office. The clapboard administrative shack was smaller than the main bunkhouses, although larger than Maria's and the other functionaries' private hovels across the yard. Its defining characteristic, however, was the large steel bar across the door. Maria knocked as she pushed it open.

"What?" she asked as she entered.

Behind its desk, the Geesler smiled. The skin it wore pulled at the seams around the mouth and jaw, revealing the pebbled hide just beneath the waxy flesh. Even when the Geesler switched skins, its throat sack pulsing gently beneath its rows of needle teeth and its honey-yellow eyes gave it away. Although it hadn't changed this covering in months and now carried a constant odor of sweet rot, the

Geesler seemed unwilling to abandon its penchant for appearing as the only male in the camp.

"Delgado," the Geesler said. "No good morning?"

"Not here."

"Sit." The Geesler flopped a hand across the desk, slamming into a stack of requisition papers and gesturing towards the chair.

Maria sat.

"We still need hygiene products," Maria said. "Pads and tampons, if you can get them."

"Oh?" The Geesler smiled and flapped its corpse-flesh hand across the table until it gripped a pen. Without looking, it made a crude pantomime of writing down Maria's request. "Anything else?"

"If you're filling out requisition forms," she said, "we could use more toilet paper."

"Shut up." The Geesler frowned, stretching its skin mask at the right corner of the mouth. It swiped its puppet hand across the desk, spreading out a heap of ragged toilet paper slips filled with messily written aphorisms about body images and/or rebellion. "What the fuck are these?"

"More subversive messages?" Maria noticed there were no pink slips among the scraps.

"Don't get smart," the Geesler said. "You were supposed to stop them, but they keep showing up near your charges."

"I'm working on it."

"Not hard enough!" The Geesler roared and the lower jaw of its false skin tore away, flapping loose below the Geesler's quivering lips.

"Things are bad out there," the Geesler said. "I'm—"

Maria interrupted: "Bad for which side?"

"I don't see many humans around, so which side do you think?"

"I don't see many Masters, either."

The Geesler glared at her, but Maria held its gaze. Neither of them spoke.

"Like I was saying." The Geesler finally broke the silence. "I'm trying to protect you, but you—specifically you and the scrawny humans in your bunk—are disappointing the Masters. These"—it smeared its dead hands across the slips—"are causing a lot of concern."

"I'm trying," Maria said. "I just need more time."

"You don't have more time," it said. "If you can't do it, you're out." It slobbered as it leaned down, the nictitating membrane of its true eyes suckering against the false lids. "I'll get someone else."

"Who?"

"Concerned?" The Geesler shrugged. "Maybe O'Connell. It's quiet ones that have a vicious streak, you know."

"Amanda couldn't do what I do."

"Couldn't run the women down into inedible gristle and fail to find a rebellious element? You're making a strong case for your replacement."

"I'll fix it," Maria said.

"Today."

"Or?"

"You choose one of your women for me—for the Masters— tonight."

Maria swallowed. "If I don't?"

The Geesler smiled. It reached across and stroked the purple band on Maria's arm that designated her as a prisoner functionary—as one of the Geesler's representatives, protected throughout the camp in exchange for enforcing the Masters' rules. "Humans like you don't last long back in the bunks without this," it said.

"I had friends in there before you made me into this."

"Had." The Geesler snorted. "Friends, lovers, family—they'll gang up on you just the same."

"Do you think they don't like me anymore?" Maria asked.

"I think they'll kill you."

"Then I'd be free."

"Then I'd eat you." The Geesler smiled. "Thin and inconsequential bitch, though, that you are."

1. "The revolution is not an apple that falls when it is ripe. Our bodies are not up for grabs."

Maria woke early to the sun's first light pushing through the teeth of the distant mountains and into her cabin. She hit the rough planks of the floor and did push-ups until failure, then crunches until her stomach screamed. She pissed in a bucket in the corner and lay on the floor, sweating, until the sun was just high enough to read by.

She moved to her narrow desk, a luxury in the prison camp, and pulled a wad of toilet paper and a stolen nub of pencil from behind a piece of loose wood paneling. She tore off little strips and began to write half-remembered bits from a life before the war:

The revolution is not an apple . . .
Just because someone looks perfect on the outside . . .
Food is not good or bad . . .
Resistance is vain . . .
Life doesn't start 10 pounds from now . . .
All oppression creates a state of war . . .
First they ignore you . . .
My body cannot be owned . . .

She folded these up and slipped them behind her belt to secretly palm them out throughout the day. Then, rolling out more of the thin paper, she wrote the following letter:

To whoever finds this:

The end is coming soon, I think, and if there are still twenty hard women in Bunk 17 when it gets here, I'll take the credit for that along with any blame. If I were a better, stronger person I might have done it in a better, kinder way, but instead I've been writing you letters in my head every day for the last month. Letters that you'll never read, explaining why I thought I needed to be cruel. Why I worked the women until they were gristle and, if I couldn't inspire them, at least I could make myself into a thing that everyone could hate together. That I also hated everything I did, even though it gave me a purpose, too.

EIGHT AFFIRMATIONS

I wanted to tell you why I pushed you away, but it isn't safe and it isn't fair. If you could hear this and still have it in you not to hate me, and maybe you could, then none of this would work. You would always be apart from everyone else and, unless everyone is together, the Geesler wins. I don't know if there's a way back for me, but if it comes down to you—any of you, all of you—or me, I know what choice I have to make.

I'm so so so sorry. I wanted to be free with you.

M

Maria read the letter once, then tore it into pieces and swallowed them. She wiped her eyes, rose from the desk. She walked to her bed, and from the pillow case she drew the slip of pink cardstock that she had found wind-pressed against the fence two months ago and had slept on top of every night since.

"HOPE," it said in thick black letters. "The Human Army is coming."

Maria tucked it back into her pillow and then left the cabin. Out in the yard, the rising sun was reflecting brilliantly orange in the puddles across the ground and spreading like fire in the contemplation of an infinite glory. For the second time in as many days the impassive sky was cracked by a single thin contrail, the human plane that it trailed still visible but already fading away into the morning.

THE HOLLOW

OUT OF THE BLUE, JESSIE—Jessica Woods—called my office on Friday morning.

"It's been a while," she said, by which she meant years. "But I didn't know who else to call."

Growing up, we had been friendly, but never friends. When I went to college, I never even thought about whether we'd ever speak again.

"You're a lawyer, right?" Jessie asked. "And you live in a big city?" Warily, I confirmed these facts. Even though Crabtree County was only a few hours away, I'd left it behind and wanted it to stay in the rearview mirror.

Jessie said her sister Janie was in a bad way, which I took to mean drugs. "I can't fix those kinds of problems," I said. "I don't do that kind of law." My practice was estates, real and testamentary, but Jessie said she knew that.

"Janie hasn't got long," Jessie said. "And we need to make sure we pass on the Hollow."

Woods' Hollow. The familial plot was, at some distant point, a prosperous homestead until mining run-off poisoned the river. The water stagnated, crops died, and the trees became diseased, dead but still standing, shrouded in Spanish moss like veils woven by vegetable spiders. The wind moaned through their rotting trunks, the empty husks thrumming.

Children called it the Hollow Woods.

The Woodses that owned the Hollow fell fallow, too. As their land withered, money also dried up, and the family's brittle branches cracked off in accidents and suspected suicides. When I was a girl, Jessie and Janie had a mother, a father, some cousins. Now they only had each other.

Morbid curiosity and Baptist guilt made my choice. I, with some fill-in-the-blank wills and Powers of Attorney, closed the office and got on the highway.

～～～

Down the long driveway, in the clearing, the family home was being reclaimed by the Hollow. Every consumable surface was poxed with grey and green lichens. Toadstools sprouted from the doorframe, and even the windowpanes were black with mold. It looked like the house had been filled with floodwater and left to sprout.

When I saw Jessie in the flesh, I was shocked at how little was left of it, and her. She was practically mummified, as if she'd been baking in much drier climates. Drugs, I thought again.

The house abandoned, she led me to her trailer in the backyard. "Well," I said, arranging my papers, "let's gets started. What are your plans—"

A woman shuffled past outside the window. Where Jessie was burnt and withered, the other was moist and bloated. Waxy skin and dim eyes glistened in the humidity as she wobbled away.

"Is that—"

Jessie nodded and lit the first of many menthols.

My presence alleviating the caregiver's isolation, she was soon bursting with questions and, eventually, confessions. She talked all afternoon. She wanted legal authority to make decisions for Janie, and she kept saying she would pass on the Hollow, but I sensed she also wanted a permission that wasn't mine to give.

A few times, Jessie cried. I hugged her and wished I could take them both with me.

As the sun set, the Hollow animals began to stir. I recognized the sounds of an opossum's shuffling drag, an owl. Something else moved, slow and off-kilter, but after years of city living, I couldn't place it.

Finally, I'd drafted everything.

THE HOLLOW

"Janie needs to sign some things. Is she, well, lucid?"

"She has a few moments."

Jessie lit another cigarette and opened the door, calling to the darkness. Beyond her, fireflies burst with coded messages. Jessie called again.

"Oh God," she whispered. "Is it too late?"

But then into the corona of the door light, Janie Woods lumbered. And it was too late.

Arms stretched like branches, Janie went right for her sister. Janie's mottled girth collapsed into Jessie, driving them into the trailer, onto the floor in front of me.

Her face had split down the middle, a pale grey stalk protruding from the ragged hole between her blackened eyes. The crowning nodule pulsed as Jessie's screams ripped through the Hollow.

"Not me!" she wailed. "I brought her for you! Get *her*!"

But flailing wildly at the remains of her sister, Jessie's nails punctured the bulbous membrane and the globular mass exploded in a nova of spores. The dry and dusty air, a perfect amalgamation of empty space and combustible flakes, caught the spark of the cigarette that Jessie still clutched and a roll of fire engulfed her head. The stalk protruding from Janie's shattered face whipped and snapped as flames began to bloom throughout the trailer.

In the rearview mirror, the Hollow burned like a blood-red moon as I accelerated towards the highway. My heart was racing, and my head was positively splitting. I headed straight here.

AS SUMMER'S MASK SLIPS

AS SHE DROVE TO HER father's house—now hers, she supposed—Sarah knew that she still remembered those woods too well to have a chance of really losing herself in them. Still, she wanted to wander the trails and desire paths once again, and to shed her burden bit by bit like breadcrumbs in her wake. To let the forest carry it away, even if she might never find her way back to the empty home.

When she was younger, she'd spent her summers out here with her father, given free rein of the wild tract between his house and the lake below. But as she returned now, a decade later and on the cusp of autumn, it was almost a different world. She had always been back in the city with her mother by the time the seasons changed, so the unfamiliar smolder of the fall's colors around her as she drove further and further into the country made it seem as if she had caught the world in the middle of putting on, or taking off, a disguise.

In fact, she'd only been out to his house one time during a season other than summer. She'd come up during the winter for Christmas the year before she left for college. She recalled pressing her face against the living room's picture window, staring at the skeletal branches groping with their stripped fingers towards the hangnail of a moon. Just the sight had made her shiver in a way the snow on the ground never could have.

"The emptiness is beautiful, isn't it?" her father had said, but Sarah didn't think so.

For her, the summer woods were the real woods. The green and full of life woods, warm and wild. That vibrant, verdant thing was the true version and honest face.

GORDON B. WHITE

The still and hollow woods, with the early nightfall and the knuckles of the forest gripping at the bone-sliver moon, that wasn't beautiful. It was something only an old man should find beauty in. Someone nearing the end of his life, consoling himself with frozen memories for the long dark sleep of winter.

Not something for her father to say. Not yet.

The next fall Sarah went to college, then found a job, and as the seasons rolled on she visited her father less often. Then he called to say that he'd gotten sick, or rather he'd been sick for a while but was only just diagnosed. He went to the hospital, he got thin and strange, and then he died. The changes all came so quickly that it seemed to Sarah as if that spindle-man that he'd withered into had been her real father, her winter father, hidden away and biding its time. As if the man she'd loved was a seed husk that had been ginned away into something raw and wicked.

Those thoughts of the end, Sarah worried, would be the ones to take hold and define him in her memories. She knew that it was best not to dwell in morbidity, though, and instead she should plant a garden of bright summer thoughts of her father and their time together. So after the paperwork was done, she decided to return to his house with the aim of filling herself to bursting as she emptied it out. In this way, Sarah planned to gather and tend to those small sprigs of happiness, so that they might one day grow into a consolation.

But her resolve remained intact only as long as the drive from the city to the dirt road cut-off. The strength fell from her soles, through the car's floorboard, and crunched like gravel beneath the tires as she ground her way past distant neighbors, further and further towards her father's isolated cabin.

Why live in such a remote area? The question echoed across the fields as she pulled into the driveway beside his truck. It had been an adventure when she was young, but it wasn't too long before she was old enough to worry about him, not just for being so far from everyone else, but for wanting to be. Even before they knew he was sick, she would get vivid impressions, like waking dreams, of him lying in the woods or sprawled facedown in his kitchen with no one to help him. No one to find him.

AS SUMMER'S MASK SLIPS

She had tried to laugh away these fantasies, calling them ridiculous. She didn't know yet how right she was. How absurd it was to think that her father would have been fortunate enough to meet some quick and silent end.

Sarah unlocked the front door with the key she'd gotten from his belongings at the hospital. There used to be a spare beneath the planter, but when she checked it out of habit, it was empty. Inside the house, however, her father's things were everywhere. A pair of old boots lay by the door, a coat on the rack. A paperback book was propped half-open on the arm of his chair, basking in the late afternoon sun. Everything was suspended mid-moment, as if he had just stepped out and would be returning at any second As if she might suddenly hear the back door open, instead of just the chimes shivering in a breeze.

In the living room, photographs frozen behind drugstore picture frames bore silent witness as she took inventory. There was Sarah the high school senior. As a little girl on a trip to England. At her college graduation, in the last photo of her mother and her father near each other, but not together.

The banality of the milestones her father had collected filled Sarah's pockets, rooting her to the floor. As she looked from picture to picture, she realized that she was trying to pinpoint the moment when she could have seen death pushing through her father's features. When she could have seen his sick and barren self getting ready to emerge.

Even if she found it now, though, what good would it do? She couldn't go back in time to tell him, *Look, there is this* thing *inside you.* Even if she could, would it have hastened his sick self's emergence and dragged that winter out over years instead of months? Would finding it now smudge every photo of him from that point forward with the taint of her failure?

She had come to get away from these thoughts, but hadn't come far enough yet. Feeling the need for air, she exited onto the back porch and gazed out past the small yard at the wall of trees that encircled it. Although the leaves were baking away into browns and oranges, although it wasn't the forest of her young summers, it called to her just the same. It had the same rough shape and features, only just changed a little, she hoped. Time must have left her that much, certainly.

Walking out through the ankle-high and unkempt blades, a distant memory returned of how her father used to mow the lawn of the little house that they all lived in together when she was just a child. Sarah could see him standing in that fenced-in yard, drenched in sweat and the smell of cut grass. Even back then and back there, surrounded by other houses, the air prickled with the scent of the wild onions that encroached from the suburbs' small feral patches.

She remembered how the onions' roots grew all twisted together, spreading out to connect to one another at seemingly random points, but coalescing into a wild and angled whole.

Her father used to say that there were many paths to the water; she just had to pick one.

This, she thought as she entered the woods, *is how I will confront the loss. By coming at it horizontally.*

<hr>

Although the woods were altered by the years of her absence and the unfamiliar changes of fall, there was enough for Sarah to recognize her woods within it. She remembered the main path and the long walks that she and her father would take. Sometimes, on pleasant days, they would take out the old canoe he kept hidden a little up from the shoreline.

"Why don't we chain it up?" she'd asked him once as they paddled across the flat and muddy water.

"Who'd want to take this old thing?" he said. "I'm surprised it even floats." Then he shifted his weight quickly, rocking the boat just enough for Sarah to grab the sides and laugh. "Besides," he said, "nobody comes down here but you and me."

"What about them?" She pointed across the water to the small landing on the far shore. Sometimes a handful of men sat in folding chairs and held fishing poles, but never seemed to be doing much else. One time, one of them waved.

"Them?" Her father laughed. "They're too far away to do anything."

AS SUMMER'S MASK SLIPS

Even then, she'd realized that the outdoors had been such a part of his life that he'd wanted to make it a part of hers. He never said why, and with the loss still fresh she didn't want to push too hard against the still-forming scar, but maybe it was something from his own childhood. Maybe it was a place to retreat when the flat empty spaces beyond the trees became too much to bear.

But whatever woods her father had seen, they weren't hers. Her forest was only an echo of his. It was a place of memories. A place of lessons.

It was learning how to tie a knot or how to play "real" hide and seek, as he called it. It was learning how to find a trail. It was her father asking, what kind of birds are they that sing these songs? What does it mean when they all go quiet?

What does it mean when the insects go quiet, too?

When nothing makes a sound?

It came back to her quickly in the now-silent forest, how the steady buzz of woods will break for an intruder.

Behind her, somewhere between the carpet of fallen leaves and those still clinging to the branches, a stick snapped and its report shot through the still world. Sarah froze, counting the seconds as if it had been a flash of lightning and she was waiting for the thunder.

But there was nothing more.

Only one crack without another could mean that it was just a falling branch or other singular event.

Or, her father reminded her, something that doesn't want to be found.

Sarah knew what animals sounded like, and that they would only pause for a second before moving on, their unencumbered minds failing to comprehend threats that didn't immediately materialize. But even then, the insects and the birds should start right up again. Life should flow on around minor disruptions like the wind through the skirts of the branches.

It shouldn't be this still and this quiet. Not for this long.

Sarah began to walk again, trying to remember how to do it quietly. Slow steps, maybe, rolling heel to toe. Maybe toe to heel. Behind her, the lengthening shadows of the sentinel trees barely breathed in the faint wind. There was no movement yet, but she felt the weight of eyes on her, the gravity of observation.

The awkwardness of her steps struck her as abundantly absurd. As absurd as this unfounded sense of dread. As absurd as the possibility of being followed through the empty woods.

But not as absurd, she knew, as having this feeling and not doing something about it.

Further down the path, closer to the lake but away from the house, she remembered that the trail wrapped around a rock outcropping. The sharp angle would cut off the line of sight behind her and allow her a small distance, just enough to catch her breath. Beneath her quickening steps, twigs broke, and the echoes behind her made a double set of steps for an imaginary ghost of a pursuer, pushing her to move faster still.

She was embarrassed for herself, acting like a child. But she didn't slow down.

Around her, the woods seemed darker than the afternoon sun should have allowed. The thick legs of trees stood in her way, and the ground threw up root walls and bramble bolls that funneled her onwards. This should be the right path, she thought, but then why did it never seem to end? Would the next twist bring her around the safety of the outcropping, or was it hiding something else?

As she began to run, she thought how foolish she must look. Wouldn't that be just what people would expect from her father's daughter, running from shadows and barking at the walls like he had in his final days?

That was, of course, if there was nothing behind her.

Sarah flew down the path, down around the bend, and came to the hook in the trail that she'd been anticipating. Around it she ran, pressing her feet deep into the ground to make her mark, then further, further, then she leapt off the trail. The small leap carried her to a table of partially exposed stones that would hide her tracks until she could make it to a deeper leaf cover. Two giant strides then, and she was clear.

As Sarah made her way up the incline of the ground, she crouched behind the sparse cover of the brush as deftly as her youthful memories could pull her aging body. She remembered to distribute her weight on elbows and palms, knees and toes. Her palms sank into the cool, dark soil, and she remembered in her bones how to hide before she fully realized in her mind that she was doing so. And when she did realize it, when she was pressed into the ground and shadows beneath the dying overgrowth and watching over the trail from above, it struck her how ridiculous all this was.

But only if there was nothing there, of course.

Except for the percussion of her heart and the rasps of her breath, the world was silent. Everything else was silent.

Everything except the sound of breaking twigs, snapping like fingers, coming down the trail.

Down below, moving slowly with knees and elbows held high in a marionette's exaggerated gait, the man crept around the rock. A bushy black beard like a squirrel's nest bobbed with each tiptoed step. He wore a green field jacket and stained jeans, but his boots, even from the distance, were shiny and new.

Whether from the dim light or her own failing eyes, Sarah couldn't see his face clearly, but she knew she didn't know him. Unbidden, the thought that came to her was of an uncomfortable photo of her father as a young man standing next to his own father— a silver-haired and wild-eyed presence that Sarah never knew. The character below was too thin and too strange to be either of them, really, but he had the same uncanny look of being out of place and out of time.

Sarah dug her fingers into the dirt as if she could pull herself down into it and away from him. The way the man swayed like a hollow tree in an unseen breeze made her nauseous. As his loose steps carried him past her hiding place, she could tell by the way he rolled his head from side to side that he was scanning the trail.

Against her better judgment, she shut her eyes. The methodical creak of the forest underfoot continued as he meandered past. She let herself exhale slowly in the self-inflicted darkness.

The sounds stopped. The forest was a tomb again.

She opened her eyes.

A few strides beyond where she had left the path, the bearded man had stopped. *Oh please*, she thought, *oh please, keep going*. She willed him onward, as if her prayers could convince unseen hands to pluck at him, cuffs and collar, and carry him out of her life.

But he didn't move on. Instead, he bent at the waist, almost in half. Close enough to sniff the ground, Sarah thought, and to see where her footfalls ended. The lolling of his head became more agitated as he surveyed the ground, and the thinness of her defenses beneath the brush struck her in the stomach. The entire forest was thinner, weaker, than she had thought even a moment ago.

No, she thought, *no, no, no*.

Like birdsong in the silence, her thoughts seemed to pierce the still world around her, and the man stopped. As he drew himself back to his full and unsteady height, Sarah recognized the look of someone who felt the pressure of hidden eyes.

He turned his head first, his body following. He looked back the way he had come, then to the downhill slope off the trail, towards the lake and away from Sarah. Then, rolling like a searchlight, he turned towards the uphill slope, towards Sarah and her father's house beyond.

Calm, she thought, *just be calm*. Maybe he was a neighbor, or a hunter, or a fisher, or even a meter man. Maybe he thought she was an intruder, or that she was lost. Maybe he was here to help. What other reason could there be?

She should stand up, then. She should call to him.

But she didn't. Instead, she watched as he raised his long, pale fingers to his face. She watched as he slowly peeled away his beard and crumpled it beneath deft, insectile movements before pressing the now abandoned disguise into a jacket pocket. Through the dimming light-dappled shade, Sarah could see the smile that split his naked face.

The man lowered onto all fours in the middle of the trail. It wasn't necessarily animalistic, but an exaggerated style of crawling that her father had once tried to teach her. One for cover and for quickness, for stalking and passing undetected.

Then he moved, scurrying into the undergrowth on Sarah's side of the trail and disappearing into the thin vegetation. The leaves whispered in his wake, spreading like the ripples from the canoe's prow as it cut the water. But that momentary disturbance faded, and then the breeze began to blow.

Below her on the hill, she heard the fallen leaves shiver. But if it was the man, bent over and scuttling on all fours, or the reawakened wind worrying the ground, she didn't know. The birds and the bugs were still catatonic, but the rest of the world seemed positively cacophonous as every creak and crinkle in the dead and dried woods around her seemed to cry at once.

Behind her, further up the slope, was her father's house. The house with doors and windows and locks. She knew the general direction was back towards the setting sun, but there was no direct path from here. She would have to stumble towards it, groping back for its safety.

Down the slope was the lake. More than one path to the water, as her father had said, and all of it was downhill. That way was a sure thing, the slopes all leading into a single depression and, from there, to her father's canoe on the embankment's high edge. But beyond that was the flat and empty water. Maybe there were fishermen, though, in their own boats or even on the distant landing, but she didn't know. There could be anything out there.

Small stones dug into her hands and legs. She became very aware of the fragility of the shell of the bush surrounding her. She had to make a choice, but which way to go? The house, of course, was clearly the safest and most familiar destination.

She would rise and turn and slowly, very slowly, begin to make her way back. If she could just get high enough, get close enough, she could find her way back and lock herself in.

But then the leaves rustled behind her on the hill, maybe fifteen, twenty feet away. They whispered to her of something circling around, cutting her off.

It was humming a song.

So Sarah ran. She burst through the flimsy concealment and sprinted down the slope, surrendering to gravity as it pulled her away from the noise between her and the house. She may have screamed, but she couldn't tell.

The velocity of terror guided her acceleration around trees and over stones. She stumbled as branches clawed at her clothes, her face, her hair. Everything in that forest seemed to drop its final pretense at summer and grasp with raw splinter fingers to hold her back, to never let her leave.

But she refused.

As she ran, her feet caught on the bones of bedrock that pierced the earth's soft old skin. The granite teeth of the ravine bit at her, the years having pulled back the soil to reveal the colossal skull of the world that had always been hiding beneath. She burst through clots of dry kindling and tore past an uprooted tree that squirmed with ten thousand legs in the gathering shadows. Down she ran, towards the end of the forest and the rim of the lake below.

She couldn't hear anything above her own thrashing, but she knew that the man was still behind her. She knew, in her deepest heart, that he was dancing down the hill like a spider, the rest of his disguises falling off of him like the autumn leaves.

Oh please, Sarah thought or even said, *please let it still be there. Let the canoe be there and let it not be chained. Of all the things that time has made strange and taken from me, please let it have left me just this one.*

And there it was, unclaimed by the years, perching on the lip of the embankment as if it were waiting to set off for the horizon's empty edge. Without breaking stride, Sarah gripped the bow, wrenching it down the slope and across the short and rocky bank. It groaned and gasped, but neither the nails of the undergrowth nor the teeth-sharp stones could hold her back as she flung it and herself out into the lake's cold and black expanse.

Her pants soaked through to her calves, her knees. Sarah shivered as she hoisted herself into the canoe, rocking wildly, then grabbed the paddle and smashed it against the dull water, beating her way further out into the empty spread.

She knew it wasn't very deep, as far as lakes go, but it looped around bends and inlets that spread like crooked fingers along the shore. On the farthest side, the fishermen's landing pushed out into the stagnant mirror of water, away from the woods and the pursuer, but away from the house, as well. Far away from the doors and the walls and any safety she could have found barricading herself in her father's old homestead.

But just then, and for just a moment, the serenity of the lake took Sarah like a drug. For just a moment she forgot the frenzy of the last few minutes. She forgot the havoc of the last few months, of all the death all around.

"How could anything ever be wrong out here?" her father had asked her once. Years ago, under the clear blue sky and unblemished sun, with the strong summer forest cradling them in its palm, she couldn't disagree.

But now, with the wilting trees gripping the black lake under the bruising sky and the sun setting behind the house in the distance, she didn't know how it could ever be otherwise. She stared at the golds and reds of the forest, and it seemed as if that whole shore behind her was burning with the dying foliage, giving off the smoke of the night. She could never go back; she knew that now.

She turned to look at the distant landing, but there wasn't a light or a soul to be seen. Of course it was empty. *No one ever comes down here but you and me*, her father had said. It was too late in the season, and surely too late in the day, and there was nothing on that far side but an empty shore and uncertain terrain. Many paths leading from the water, she imagined, but she didn't know where to.

So Sarah laughed. Laughed at the darkening plateau of the pond. Laughed at the absurdity and at herself and at the absolute isolation reflected back at her on every side.

And as she laughed, as she looked back to the silent immolation of the autumn leaves and the sunset consuming her father's house and the woods behind her, the man emerged onto the shore. Like the memory of a picture, his details were smeared beneath dusk's thumb.

She watched as he stooped to pick up fist-sized rocks from the water line. She watched him stuff them into the pockets of his field jacket.

Even now, as the darkness won the sky, she saw his glistening smile as his shiny boots broke the water's mirror surface. He smiled as he went in past his knees, past his stomach, past his chin. His head disappeared without any bubbles, leaving only a gentle ring of ripples that spread like the whisper of the leaves before it vanished.

The water was still again, its murky shadows concealing fish and driftwood and a grinning man and who could ever know what else. Sarah was alone here, in the wide spread of nothing, with only that thin membrane between her and that hidden depth and everything within it.

Sarah dug her paddle's blade into the waters and pushed forward, towards the far and darkening shore.

THE MEATBAG VARIATIONS

ALICIA'S ART IS SOMETHING CLOSE to dying. She has given herself just one more month to finalize her performance and display it at her studio space's Winter Showcase. If she can't do it, she promises herself, then it's over for good.

Alicia is a dancer, a performer, and her art is not really dying, of course, but a movement series where she sprawls out of a chair or off a stool, careens across the boards, and then lies there on the stage floor for a while. When she's perfected it, music might play or other dancers may run their choreography or maybe the audience will just sit and stare, but right now she's working through all the possible motions. Each time she's exploring the fall a little differently and coming at that final moment from every possible angle. She's seeing which of her dozens of variations is the ultimate way to become the Meatbag.

Alicia leaves her practice at the studio one day, sweating despite the chill, beneath layers of clothes that will better befit the kind of cold she'll be when her heart stops beating. That's how she feels that she must always go out into the world, dressed for that point when either her work is done or she finally succumbs to the suffocations of life—her relationship, her job, all the pressures on her heart and her time that keep her from truly practicing. Her art is suffering.

Above her, the sky is striped in the violent bruise and citrus hues that soak early winter's premature evenings. She's running late; Danny will be waiting at home and will not be pleased. Alicia shivers. The sun's surrender behind the horizon's black teeth has left the streets and alleys swallowed in blue shadow. The streetlights' timers have yet to click on. In the darkness, though, a person is leaning against the warehouse-cum-performance space's furthest corner.

At first, the bulk of the silhouette is misshapen in a way that breaks up the recognizable lines that read "human." Like Alicia, this figure is also dressed too much and in too many layers—better suited for a world in which they'll never move quickly, their heart rate will never rise, they'll never go indoors. It is, the thought occurs to Alicia's artist brain, an outfit for a reptile or a hibernating bear. A great bearded dragon in an anorak presents itself to her mind's eye.

Around here, one might find a few loft dwellers betting on gentrification, a few lingering self-storage concerns, and the odd artist collective, such as the New High Stage that Alicia has just locked up for the night, but the NHS is the only active entity on this particular block. The rest are ghost buildings and empty lots that still bear the scars and faded signage of their past lives. There is no reason to be on this corner other than the theater.

"Hello?" Alicia calls to the figure. "Are you waiting for someone?"

It turns to her and, snuggled in the depths of the hood, Alicia sees her own face looking back at her. It doesn't blink, but its lips tilt on the knife-edge of a smile.

Alicia entertains every notion on the spectrum from mad to maddest as she sprints towards home. Her artist brain works overtime, spinning up and overheating: a hallucination from overwork; an elaborate prank; a tumor; a fancy; a ghost; a mistake. She knows what it really is, though. She's seen it in the digital records of workshop performances and self-shot cellphone footage of her practice.

It is the Meatbag come to life.

The Meatbag is a longstanding artistic preoccupation. It's an inchoate aesthetic concept that Alicia wrestles into shape one tumble and spill onto the floor at a time, trying to find that point of embodiment and abandonment. It's a recurring theme in her work, no more. No more. Now it is behind her.

THE MEATBAG VARIATIONS

Madness, Alicia thinks. Deserves another look, she also thinks, although the grammar of the mind jumbles the sentence. Two blocks east, then she turns north for one, then back west for three, circling the New High Stage. She's coming up on it from behind, but when she gets back on the level of the theater the corner is empty. The figure has moved on, although it has left a trace: the heaviest of the double's outer layers lies cast off like a chrysalis on the corner. Further down the block, along the path that Alicia had originally run, she sees other items of clothing litter the sidewalk.

It occurs to Alicia that the Meatbag, even now, even naked, is creeping up behind her. She does not turn around to see, but briskly walks away. She skirts the discarded jacket and sweaters and scarves on the pavement as if they're alive.

The lights are on in the ground-floor apartment that Danny and Alicia share on Queen Charlotte Avenue. As Alicia passes by on the way to the building's entrance, she peers through the thin intrusion where the slats of the patio door's vertical blinds don't quite reach the wall, and she sees Danny's boots, his legs, his hands curled like stones on his thighs. The angle is too sharp to see Danny's face, but Alicia knows the dark twist of it.

She can't go home like this. She walks past the apartment and then crosses the street to begin a slow loop back on the other side, unable to conceive of any plan other than the delay. But it's there, standing across the street and staring at the home she cannot enter, that Alicia sees the Meatbag coming down the other side of the street, towards her building. It's wearing Alicia's same outer coat and pants, and as it passes in and out of the orange glow of the streetlights, its unperturbed expression is masked in shadow one moment and revealed the next. Frozen, Alicia watches the gait of the thing, noting how it mirrors the same splay in her own step from the same little hitch of a chronically tight IT band.

The Meatbag doesn't even look at her as it pulls out a keychain with the same copper bear-face bottle opener and heads into the building. Alicia watches through the glass as the Meatbag checks the mail, looks at the names on the packages left along the wall, then disappears around the corner. She runs across the street, back to the position where she can see that sliver of what's inside her apartment. From here, she can see the door and watches it open, the Meatbag standing there, smiling in her vacant way.

Although Alicia can't hear the conversation, she knows the lines like a precisely choreographed routine. She can hear the silent music of Danny's accusations as he rises. A faint shout makes it through the wall and Alicia, even outside of the realm of awareness, flinches. The Meatbag, however, does not. It smiles and takes the scorn, even as it rises to something Alicia can see from the outside might be called abuse.

In a familiar motion, Danny grabs the Meatbag but, unlike Alicia, it goes willingly, arms swinging loosely. Danny shoves it and it drifts backward, almost elegantly, into the refrigerator. The magnetic fruits tremble and fall, the picture of them on vacation in San Francisco sliding to the floor like a leaf on the breeze. Yet the Meatbag doesn't respond.

Danny's anger has exerted itself and, it seems, without Alicia to further antagonize him through self-assertion, it's done so quicker than before. He gives up and returns to the couch, once more leaving only his boots in the strip of visibility. The Meatbag disappears behind the curtain, towards the kitchen.

Twenty minutes later and Alicia is standing in the elbow of the interior hallway before her door, unsure of what to do. Then the door opens and the Meatbag comes out dressed in her jacket, a bulging sack of garbage in hand, and disappears down the stairwell to the garage and dumpsters below. Alicia slips inside the apartment and locks the door. From the couch Danny looks up.

"That was quick," he says. "See? You can be on time, if you want."

Alicia merely nods. She takes off her jacket and sits down beside Danny. He drops a hand onto the back of Alicia's neck and squeezes as if he were trying to work his fingers into a sock puppet.

"You're all tense," Danny says as he kneads her. "You need to learn to calm down."

THE MEATBAG VARIATIONS

Gordon, Alicia's supervisor during the Wednesday morning shift at Café Fetch, bangs an espresso portafilter against the knock bar, jarring her back to the present. One of the soporific dogs that the café tolerates because of its name, and despite the health codes, yawns lazily. Alicia had been thinking about last night and what she saw. She's thinking about how to work it into her ongoing artistic project.

"I asked, are you unhappy?" Gordon repeats.

Alicia pauses before answering. "Not more than other people, I don't think," she says. "But who ever knows what anyone else is thinking or feeling, right? It would be wrong to complain, I mean."

Gordon stares at her. "I meant, like, working here."

"Oh. No."

"Then pep up a little, okay?" His hand brushes against her arm and she twists out of range, the connection like a shock.

"What's your deal?" he says.

"Sorry," Alicia says, already wondering why she was apologizing and if it was an overreaction. "I just thought you had something hot."

Gordon turns back to the grinder, shaking his head. Alicia wonders what it would have looked like to an impartial observer. She would have liked to see the motions and the movements from a perspective outside of her own. She would have liked to incorporate it into her performance, which now, now that she really considers it, seems to be about damage.

Alicia is outside, dumping a bulging sack of used filters and freezer-burned quiches into the green composting bin behind Café Fetch when she hears the footsteps echoing from the alley. The sky is cold and clear, the winter sun sparkles like a gemstone, and there is no obscurity or confusion. The Meatbag is approaching.

It wears the same black apron tied around its waist, with the same ghostly palm print of powdered sugar from Alicia's mishap in the pastry case. Alicia feels the lock of hair that has slipped from behind her ear press against her forehead as she sees the mirrored strands on the Meatbag. The two of them are, as far as Alicia can tell, identical except for one important difference: The Meatbag bears it all like a sphinx, lips fixed and eyes staring in the middle distance.

A bottle fly rises from the compost bin's open lid and in its frantic, drunken flight careens into the Meatbag's face and sticks to its cheek. As her double draws near, Alicia watches the fly rub its greedy legs together as if saying grace and then kiss the wet of the Meatbag's eye. The Meatbag never even blinks. Instead it turns and enters Café Fetch through the back, the breeze from the swinging door finally shooing the fly away.

"You have a problem out there?" Alicia hears Gordon ask as the door swings shut. Whatever is said next, however, it's too faint to pass through.

Day by day, Alicia surrenders every disagreeable and painful aspect of her life to the Meatbag so that she can concentrate on the upcoming Winter Showcase. When she wakes in the morning, Danny is already gone as usual, but now the Meatbag is in the bathroom doing hair and make-up. The dummy is jostled and pinched on the bus downtown, all while Alicia watches from the seat in the back, jotting down how the Meatbag fidgets and twists. It goes to work, it runs its errands, it comes home at night to Danny without laughing or crying. Its rigid face is blank but its body, Alicia is dazzled to observe, its body reacts to and records everything.

Through her observations, Alicia begins to decipher where her performances at the NHS must have failed. On stage she's only been playing at pain, but she actually resists it and hides herself from the full brunt. The Meatbag, though, gives itself over to every abuse without complaint.

Alicia watches the Meatbag for hours on end, the nub of a pencil and a drugstore sketchpad in hand, trying to the capture the angles and lines of the Meatbag in distress. She traces the slope of the Meatbag's spine as it labors to the dumpster under heavy sacks of café garbage and how its hand flutters like a wounded bird when the milk steamer scalds it. A twist of the hip when Gordon touches the small of its back, or the hunch of the shoulders when Danny shouts; Alicia watches from the distance to recreate the curves of pain in the Meatbag's frame and figure when the days insult it again and again.

Alicia is making art. Through their separation she is turning the Meatbag's suffering into motion; she is linking the croquis gestures in a chain of movements, all of which will culminate in a final demonstration she is calling "The Meatbag Variations."

Even with the Meatbag as a buffer, Alicia is still an ever-expanding diagram of injuries that she doesn't remember receiving. Danny says she must bruise herself by flailing in her sleep, but his tone suggests he thinks she's accusing him. She's not, though. This time, she thinks, it must be the Meatbag.

Each night, Alicia lies in bed and waits for Danny's breathing to fall into the shallow rhythm of his sleep even while the mattress and box spring shift beneath them as the Meatbag repositions itself under the bed. When Alicia's eyes have been closed long enough that even the Meatbag must think she's asleep, Alicia hears the rasp of its back as it worms out from below. She feels the static tingle of its presence as it hovers above her. Alicia wants to wait it out, she thinks, to see how it works, but whether by exhaustion or avoidance, sleep always touches Alicia before the Meatbag does. Inevitably, she falls.

Alicia dreams, however, that the Meatbag draws broken nails across her skin, leaving twinned sets of scratches. Its cold lips, never quite smiling, move along Alicia's thighs and arms, her belly, pressing down to suck the blood up through the layers of spongy flesh, leaving sympathetic bruises just beneath the skin.

At night, she believes, the Meatbag makes Alicia match. However it happens, the Meatbag spares her the pain but leaves her the scars. Alicia pretends to sleep through it.

From a distance, at least, the Meatbag is a perfect mimic—its physicality, its stage presence, are impeccable—yet there is one aspect that Alicia cannot observe. After several days, though, it occurs to her that at some point the Meatbag must speak, if only to answer questions or take directions, but of course Alicia herself is always too far away to hear.

Even if she could get close enough to the Meatbag without tipping off the people around her, however, Alicia fears hearing its voice. There are two possibilities that she can acknowledge: First, that it sounds like her, and that she'll hear her own voice playing back to her, but without the familiar reverberations of the bones in her head. The uncanny distance between speech and recording, magnified and in real time, is a disorienting prospect.

The second possibility, of course, is that it doesn't sound like her. It's something altogether alien that she has let take over her life, and no one in her world notices or cares.

There is a third possibility, too, although Alicia refuses to think it and presses it down whenever it surfaces: People prefer the silent, compliant Meatbag to Alicia. That they know it isn't her, but they're happy.

～～

With only two weeks to go until the Winter Showcase, Alicia workshops the Meatbag Variations for a few other artists that are close to friends, but who offer the kind of cutting commentary that's almost always too close to true to be helpful. Still, one of the performance notes—"Not enough escalation, just variation"—sticks in the craw of Alicia's mind. Her artist brain swallows around it, coughing and hacking, until one day it spits out the answer: The Meatbag's pain has been too pedestrian.

With time running short before Alicia's drop-dead point at the Winter Showcase, how can she escalate the suffering into feeling? There are a few ways that occur to her, although all of them require a more direct hand than Alicia has taken so far. There are two possibilities: First, that she directly inflict the suffering on the Meatbag herself. Second, that she lead the Meatbag into more and more dangerous situations.

There is a third possibility, too, although Alicia refuses to think it and presses it down whenever it surfaces.

THE MEATBAG VARIATIONS

Here is how the first possibility plays out:

Alicia sees the Meatbag often enough that she could injure it at any point she wants. Passing Alicia in the hallway to take the brunt of Danny's upset, she could grab the Meatbag's arm and drag a key across it, watch it recoil at the jagged wound. Waiting for the bus in the rain, Alicia could push the Meatbag out in front as the vehicle skids to a stop, just enough for it to clip the Meatbag and spin it like a pinwheel. She could go into Café Fetch and throw hot coffee in its face. She could burn it with a hair curler. She could attack it and beat it and scrape it and cut it and kill it, maybe, maybe not. But doing so would do all that to herself.

At night, when the Meatbag worms out from beneath her bed and its chilly fingers and cold lips hover just above her body, Alicia doesn't want to die. Every time she picks up an implement to inflict some sort of major destruction upon the Meatbag, she instead pictures it against her flesh, against her bones. She can't bring herself to do that.

Moreover, she thinks, no one wants to see an artist committing actual self-harm. They want the pain and they want the motions and the resolution, but not the overt masochism.

Here is how the second possibility plays out:

Alicia has a lifetime's worth of practice putting herself into harm's way, so it's easy to fall back into these patterns without too much effort. The pressure of the upcoming Showcase performance also helps dramatically. Danny is out of town, and so Alicia goes to bars. She stays late. She drinks a lot and then, when she feels that prickle at the back of her neck that she has learned indicates that danger—and the Meatbag—is near, she drinks some more. Then she hides in the women's restroom and waits until she can poke her head out to see—not herself, but her double, her crash test dummy—the Meatbag out there on the stool. She waits and she observes.

It finally happens two nights before the Showcase. When it does,

149

Alicia doesn't do anything different to precipitate the event. She doesn't go to a different part of town or wear anything for the Meatbag to copy that she wouldn't wear herself. She doesn't drink more to incapacitate the Meatbag, or openly flirt with men. She merely drinks her few cocktails and sits alone on her stool, not looking like a monster, and when the prickle on her neck hits, she doesn't even order another. She just rises and goes to the restroom.

When she returns, the Meatbag is sitting at the bar. The man next to it has an arm around the Meatbag's mid-back—a middle place not so controlling as the shoulder or as intimate as the hips. Alicia leans against the far wall and watches as the stranger draws the thing that looks like her closer. Maybe tonight, although the thought is a little fuzzy, she'll get the final movement in her piece.

The mirror behind the bar offers Alicia a widescreen view of the rough pretense of courtship to which the man subjects the Meatbag. He leans on it, squeezes it, puts his mouth up next to its ear and presses his moist words directly into its soft curves. Across the mirror's divide Alicia watches the Meatbag's blank face as the man waits for an answer and, getting none, closes back in and sucks the Meatbag's lobe between his lips.

Alicia maneuvers herself to better glimpse the Meatbag's face. She needs something, anything. A twist of the lips, a furrow of the brow, a vein that throbs—anything that would suggest a depth of feeling beyond just physicality.

It is, her artist brain pauses to think, a scene worthy of a painting. Two identical women's faces: One in the foreground, staring straight into its own empty gaze as the lush beside her drips onto her shoulder, hand disappearing suggestively below the frame. The other is distant, relegated to the upper corner in the way Old Masters depicted cherubs or personified thoughts, but also peering straight ahead and utterly alone. If someone slashed out those two swatches of canvas and showed them to Alicia, she wouldn't be able to tell them apart.

Then Alicia is up. She's moving through space and against time, passing around the other bodies in motion, harnessing all the chaos that threatens to erupt from her and channeling it towards the Meatbag and the man beside her.

THE MEATBAG VARIATIONS

"Leave me alone." Alicia grabs the Meatbag by the arm and jerks it from the stool. The hole its sudden absence leaves in the net of the stranger's arms sets him off balance, and he tips over before catching himself against the bar.

"Bitch," he shouts as Alicia drags the characteristically silent Meatbag towards the door.

~~~

This is how the third possibility plays out:

Hooked arm in arm, Alicia guides the Meatbag home. At the door she pauses, fishing for keys in her bag, afraid to let the Meatbag go for even a second, lest it slip away down the hall or melt into the air in one of its great vanishing acts. She must, though, and so she lets go—just for a moment—to find her keychain with the bear face and open the door.

Alicia turns around, expecting to be alone. But no. Clasping her double by the hand, Alicia opens the door and pulls the body behind her across the threshold.

Alicia takes the Meatbag into the bathroom, and for a moment they stand side-by-side in the mirror over the sink, too identical to even be twins. She exhales, clenches her diaphragm to hold that lack of breath deep inside her, wills herself to stop moving and her heart to stop beating. The world swims in and out, reflected strangely, and for a second Alicia cannot tell which woman in the mirror is her and which is not. Then she exhales and finds herself once more.

With cotton pads dipped in micellar water, Alicia swabs off her own makeup and then makes the Meatbag match. She ties their hair back and lathers up both their faces until they're masked by bubbles, then she gently scrubs them both clean. She brushes her own teeth, rinses the bristles clean and works out the months of hardened paste near the base, then hands it to her double to do the same. When it finishes rinsing, spitting, and cleaning, the Meatbag places the brush back in the holder and stands like a soldier waiting for orders.

When Alicia steers it towards the bedroom, the Meatbag crouches down on its hands and knees, crawling like an insect towards the space between the bed and the floor. Alicia grabs it by the shoulder, arresting its movement. With gentle pressure, she pulls it back and stands it up again. If the Meatbag is surprised, it gives no indication.

Instead, Alicia undresses the Meatbag. Seeing it naked before her, there is no prurient thought, not even a twinge of the erotic, only the familiar. Every freckle and blemish, every scab and scrape, the curve of her legs that she likes and the paunch around her hips that she hates—all of it is hers. Her artist brain wants to abstract it, to view it as a system of shapes and shades, lines of potential energy to be harnessed into motion, but it isn't that. Alicia sees that now.

She dresses the Meatbag in a soft t-shirt and hospital scrub pajama bottoms; then Alicia makes herself match. She guides them both into bed, beneath the blanket, and they both roll on their left side, which Alicia knows will tweak their hips but will help them to avoid acid reflux after a night of drinking.

Facing her double's back—she can no longer think of it as the Meatbag—Alicia watches her side rise and fall with each breath. She had never noticed her breathing before. Alicia inches across the gap between them, and wraps her arm around her ribs. She feels the forms of bone and muscle moving with the breath and the heartbeat they contain. She buries her face against her back, nestling it between her shoulder blades. She kisses her through the shirt as she would a sister. She can smell her skin.

⚓︎

The heavy curtains of the New High Stage divide Alicia from her audience as she waits for her cue. The quality of the air changes as her track comes on and the pregnancy of recorded silence before the beat begins to fill the room. Alicia affords herself only a single glance at the risers out beyond the footlights. They are, uncharacteristically, full.

Then the music starts, and she's leaving the safety of the backdrop. She is alone on the stage, empty except for the props of chair, stool, and box. In this, the first performance of the final version of the Meatbag Variations, Alicia has foregone the presence of an assistant. Partly out of her failure to choreograph a partner, but mostly out of her desire not to be acted on by outside forces but to perform in her own skin, she is dancing by herself.

THE MEATBAG VARIATIONS

She moves into the chair; then the bass hits and she's out of it, cartwheeling elbows and knees across the floor in a movement recorded from the Meatbag. She lies there, eyes closed, listening for the next beat. Then she is up and moving to the next position.

Across the floorboards, from station to station, Alicia runs through the Meatbag's variations. She slumps and skitters, she limps and tumbles. She falls and lies there and then rises again with the music. She bounces and slaps across the stage as she connects the dots of the bruises that the Meatbag left behind, inscribing through spaces all those instances of pain into a line and then a curve and then a picture of all she has been through. She hits the floor—again, again, again. She rises—again, again.

Then the music stops and Alicia remains on the floor, limbs sprawled and spine twisted, her eyes closed. The lights go out and the stage goes dark, the red curtain of illumination through her eyelids turns black, and she can feel the toll of the performance ringing through her body. The resonance of her jarred bones pulses through her strained joints. The blood of old bruises made new begins pooling beneath her skin.

She waits, but there is only silence. Through the slit of a single open eye, Alicia looks at the crowd. Now adjusted to the darkness, she can see them all: every stone-still face that watches her is hers; every body in the seats is hers.

They are all the Meatbag.

Alicia rises even as her body resists. The spotlight clicks back on and pins her to the stage before the Meatbags, every one of the dozens of variations of which sits in anticipation. They are waiting, Alicia realizes, for the final movement. They don't want their pain merely replayed and reflected back at them—they want it transformed.

Alicia takes a deep breath, spreads her aching muscles and bones from inside, willing herself to deliver the final movement. She holds it, frozen under all of her eyes, but nothing is coming. Her vision blurs, and only when Alicia finally gasps in exhalation does she realize she is crying.

"I'm so sorry," she says to the crowd through now-heaving sobs. "I'm not sure how."

All the pain, all the observing and recording, she's ready to let it go but has nothing to put in its place. Head bowed, Alicia turns to run back to the safety of the crimson curtains, but a great and concerted rustling, like a heavy beast shuffling to its feet, stops her. She hesitates, afraid that if she turns to look, the horde of her abused stand-ins will fall upon her like raving maenads. Still, she owes them something, anything.

Alicia wipes her eyes, then turns. In the front row of risers, each Meatbag has slid over just a little, and the cumulative movement has left room enough for one more on the edge. The double on the end pats the empty seat in invitation.

Alicia sniffles as she steps off the stage and leaves the spotlight, descending on bare feet into the darkness. She sits down in the empty space alongside her silent witnesses. The lights dim again, but instead of the curtains opening, from beside Alicia, a warm hand slips into hers and squeezes gently. Another pats her on the shoulder. Eyes still glistening and nose still running, Alicia smiles. Without looking back, she knows the rows behind her follow suit, as together they complete the Meatbag Variations' final movement.

BIRDS OF PASSAGE

IF I DIDN'T INHERIT MY father's natural instinct for adventure, it was drummed into me steadily enough by the time I was a young man that you wouldn't have been able to tell the difference. *If you don't go looking for adventure*, he would say, *adventure will come looking for you.* Over the years, I got so used to the counter-programming against my inborn tendency towards the comfort of safety that I wonder—if left to my own natural limits—would I have turned out differently? Are there other dimensions with less driven, but perhaps more content, versions of me? I've thought about that a lot since my father died.

My father and I had plenty of what he would call "adventures," even though we sometimes disagreed on what qualified. Road trip to the mountains and across state lines? Sure, that counted. Pushing his broken car to the dealership and walking home? Not in my book. Nowadays, although I wouldn't trade any of them for the world, the years have smudged away most of our individual adventures. However, I will never forget Cotner's Creek.

I was ten years old, and it was Labor Day weekend. I remember that clearly because there are only two real sections of my life: before that trip and after. If I ever were to return, I wonder if there would be a third fork, or if this is it? My father would have known, of course, but he's not likely to tell me now. It's not impossible—nothing truly is—but it's very unlikely.

We'd spent the week before preparing for the trip. In retrospect, I realize now how much of it had been planned in advance, but the way that my father involved me made it seem as much my trip as his; it was as if we were equal partners stocking up for the expedition. From the way he consulted me about which canoe to rent, to the excursions up and down the supermarket aisles shopping for two days of river rations to fill the cooler that would sit between us, I seemed to have a say in every part. Finally, I thought, I was a man and my opinion mattered.

We excavated my mother's garage until we re-discovered the musty relics of sleeping bags, poncho liners, and other accouterments for camping. These were leftover things that had been squirreled away after he'd gotten married and stayed buried after he'd gotten divorced, but even their stale smells were akin to the yellowed pages of an old atlas—a reminder of adventures past and the empty spaces where still more hid. Although we had a tent, too, we agreed that we wouldn't bring it, because the forecast was clear and we wanted to sleep beneath the stars. What was the point of two men heading out into the wild only to hide from it all? We wanted to experience everything.

Because I was an equal partner in name and spirit, if not in stakes and logistics, a brackish current of trepidation and excitement swept me along. What if we got lost? What if we capsized? Where would we go to the bathroom? Were there wild animals? Would it be cold? My father laughed at all of these questions but gave me straight answers, although most of those scenarios never came to pass. What did happen, though, was something that I could never have understood how to ask. Even after we went down Cotner's Creek, I'm still not sure I can.

My mother drove us down to the bridge over Cotner's Creek, out off the interstate between Statesville and Wallace, which is near where my father grew up. The highway crosses through long fields of cash crops slit by the occasional meandering river, and further hemmed in by fingers of undeveloped forests. In the summer those fields are heavy and green, swaying under fleshy tobacco leaves or tight-lipped bolls of cotton. By the fall, however, they're in the process of being stripped bare and harrowed through for the next year's planting. It was Saturday, and she planned to pick us up further down the river the next afternoon.

She watched as my father and I off-loaded the rental canoe, our camping gear, and the Igloo chest filled with provisions. It was only years later, when she was moving in with her next husband, that I came across a snapshot she had taken that day when I wasn't looking. There I was in a bright red cap and bright orange life preserver, a figurehead on the bow of the canoe like a little ornamental torchbearer. Behind me, my father was caught in just the slightest profile, forever frozen in the act of pushing off along the winding path of water and toward the veil of trees beyond. I've looked at it many times, but I still can't read in that sliver of his face if he knew what was going to happen.

As we set out, though, in the full of morning's light, it was a grand adventure. Paddling with the river gave the sensation not so much of leaving the world behind, but of pushing further inside it. Our surroundings changed along each bend of the river, as if the banks were contorting themselves to show off every aspect as we moved deeper into its coils. Open fields gave way to trees, but then a broken-ankle turn would reveal a fenced-in yard. At times, the creek thinned out to barely a stream, but then another turn opened up to cataracts of near-whitewater rapids. No matter how many stories I'd heard from my father, watching the world switch from inhabited to primeval, from narrow and cultivated to wide and bursting with wild energy, it was seeing the shift with my own eyes that brought an understanding no story ever could. As we moved through these unfolding aspects, all united by the almost arbitrary cut of the creek through their disparate dimensions, it was as if I was moving backwards past my father's stories and into a deeper, stranger imagination.

There is one part, in particular, that sticks out to me more than any other. We had just come through a peculiarly narrow pinch of the creek and opened up into a wide, glassy pool. The water was brown but transparent for about a foot down before it clouded over, resisting the sun that punched through the grasping branches and into the shallows. Beneath us, as if the shade of our canoe was obfuscation from a higher plane, long-bodied gar swam up from the clouded depths and followed beneath us. In our shadow a new stratum of their world was presented and so they rose up, their needle noses and armored flanks primitive and unintelligible in this thin layer. I wondered if they knew that my father and I could have held gig hooks to spear them or nets to ensnare them, but that to us, in particular, they were curiosities. They had lived for decades in this river and their ancestors had for millennia been kings of this simple cut of water through the deep red banks, but even though they knew nothing of us, we could have—had we wanted—been a danger. Still, they swam and basked. They dove back deep into the blackness, and if they saw us—if our canoe and our unused armaments registered to them at all—it only gave them more freedom, allowing them to rise higher in our shadow before descending back into their depths, unable to ever properly describe to their fish wives and fish children what marvels they'd seen.

Is it any wonder, then, that as the whole world of the creek grew so gradually stranger and stranger the further we travelled—as new creatures swam up and the banks bleached from red to gray, as the trees grew crooked and vines hung like witch's hair—that I failed to appreciate the full extent of how different things truly had become?

As the day ended and the palimpsest of sunset colors and evening sounds settled around us, we found a bend in the river with a wide-open field next to it. Because it was so vast and clearly unused by other people, we set up camp further off the bank, up on a little rise. The canoe stayed below, wedged into the grey clay at the waterline and lashed to a few saplings. We spread our tarps and bedding over the dead leaves and gnarled roots, but the ground's chill still permeated up through the layers.

The night was cool, and a thin film of clouds swept back and forth across the wide, hungry sky. We were just at the point where the ground opened up into the field and the trees overhead still clung to the modesty of a few leaves, but beyond them the silver teeth of stars were starting to nibble through the bruise of the evening. Looking up, the night felt cooler to be that bright with distant fire.

We made our own fire of the thick branches already littering the ground. Although it hadn't rained in days, those long arms of wood had soaked up the moisture from the cool ground and the water below. Their bark hung like damp skin, hissing and whistling before taking the flame. Still, once we had the fire going, the cocoon of light it wove was enough to make me feel safe within its embrace.

After a day of paddling, our provisions of box juice, peel-top soup cans, and King's Hawaiian rolls were practically a feast. As usual, we talked about small things—my school, our plans for a tree house once he found a new place—but all of it took on a grave importance there by the river. It was as if we were discussing ancient things; as if our lives outside the woods had become myths that occurred centuries ago or perhaps wouldn't occur for centuries yet. Maybe it was that dislocation that unmoored my father, which sent him back down that silver thread of memory outside the firelight. Whatever the reason, he then told me a story I'd never heard before.

"When I was a boy," he began, "I grew up about fifteen miles from the bridge where we set off. You know how I've told you before about my best friend Gary? Well, he and I did this same trip that you and I are doing. Gary and I put in at the same spot—although it was a different bridge back then, an old one made of bricks that they tore down when the highway came through."

The thing about his stories, I've come to realize, is that I never could quite tell when they were true and when they just felt that way. They all felt real enough then and, in time, all of the past takes on that same grain that blurs truth and untruth, so the only thing I guess that really matters is who remembers it and how it felt to hear.

He went on: "When Gary and I made this trip, though, it was summer. It was so humid that year, so damp in the air, that do you remember that little waterfall in the rapids we took after lunch? Well, he and I did the same thing, but we got a good foot further past the edge before we tipped over because the canoe was paddling through that steamy air."

"Was it the same as it is now, though?" I asked. "Because it feels, maybe, strange?"

I couldn't quite put what I felt into words, but from the slight drip of a frown that escaped him, I could tell he knew what I meant, but that he hadn't been planning on taking his story down this path. At least, not yet.

"Yes." He swallowed hard and looked at me with the steel glint that meant that this was man talk. No anger, no fear, but still deathly serious. "I think that's why I brought you here."

"This place is . . ." He fluttered his hand for a moment, trying to conjure the right word out of the fire. "It's a soft place, I think. It isn't quite here, and isn't quite there. There aren't people and there aren't roads, but you can feel that something more surrounds us."

It took me a moment to respond. I held a paper towel napkin in my hands, which I balled and unrolled to an unheard rhythm. He was right, or at least it felt like he was right, because there I could also feel something under that black dome of sky and all the million fly specks of distant light above us that peered through and then were swept away in the current of clouds. Some enormousness that seemed to both pull me up and press me down at the same time. Out in the distance, the soft yellow bruise of light pollution over far-off cities seemed like dapples of light on the river bottom, obscured by layers of some other medium that my father and I were now suspended in, just like gar in the river.

"I feel it," I said, although the description of it wouldn't come to me for years. But the way I said it, my dad knew. He nodded.

"I don't know what you'd call it," he finally said. With a slender stick, he prodded the embers on our low fire and sent the shadows skipping like water bugs. "Maybe the bigness of nature, or a great spirituality. Something, though, you don't feel at home."

He looked out for a moment at the darkness, at the stars above. "Sometimes," he said, "I think about all the possible worlds we could have lived in, but that we're in the one that makes you my son and me your father and brings us here. It sounds stupid"—he paused— "but sometimes I look at you and I think, 'Are you real?'"

"Yeah," I said. He laughed and I smiled, even though I don't know if he saw me do it, there in the shadow just beyond the fire's light. For a while, we just sat and listened to the world.

"Do you feel it everywhere?" I eventually asked, meaning the thing he had talked about and meaning everywhere outdoors; but even though I didn't clarify, my father knew. He and I shared a wavelength like that.

"Maybe if you try real hard, but I've never felt it quite like I feel it here." He leaned back, caught between the orange light below and the silver light above. "Just think," he went on, "that outside of our fire light, it's miles to the nearest town. Straight up and out above us, for millions of miles, is nothing but empty space. Beneath our skin, hidden from sight, run rivers of blood and cells and atoms and, deeper still, the empty space between them. You and I and everything else are just thin layers between space and distances, just skins between mysteries we could never know."

He stopped, probably wondering if he'd gone too far or said too much. Then he looked at me and asked, "Are you scared?"

"No," I said, "but it is a little scary."

"Yeah," he nodded as he spoke, "but it's also kind of awesome."

As if to underscore the end of that thread, I threw my crumpled napkin into the fire. I watched, however, as the edges caught the ember, glowing and curling up at the tips like wings. It must have been shaped just right by the chaotic worrying—a broken bird accidentally birthed through dirty origami—because the folds caught the warm air beneath them, and it was buoyed up, burning, into flight. Up over the fire, we watched it rise, catching feathers of flame as it rose, shrinking and consuming itself from the outside in as it drafted up towards the stars. All told, it couldn't have taken more than a few seconds, but in my mind there is a forever-playing slow-motion shot of the paper phoenix, rising up into the blackness and fading from view—too far, too small, too burned—until it seemed to be swallowed into the night beyond us.

We sat in silence for a moment after it vanished, listening to the wood whisper in its combustion and the crickets sing along. Behind us, the water chuckled softly and, on the other side, the great open field lay quiet in the starlight. Everything just beyond the fire was bluer than the deepest water and, beyond that, only black.

As my eyes grew accustomed to the gloaming, however, a single point of light emerged in the distance. Seeing it too, my father stood up and pointed across the field. Despite the stars above, the darkness was like a curtain of black wool pulled from the ground to the trees, but across from us, near where I remembered the opposite tree line being, there was a glow. It was faint, but pushing through the cover like a hot vein beneath night's scales.

"Is that a fire?" I asked, but I knew it was. Immediately, I recalled the rising flame from our fire and had visions of a soft coal falling across the field, catching hold there on the ground. "Did we do that?"

"I don't think so," my father replied. "It looks too big, and it's too damp for anything to catch from that little spark."

"Is it other people?" My imagination again went to the other side, now peering around at the possible figures surrounding that distant beacon. I had thought that we were far from town, and it seemed unlikely that anyone else would find the same adventure here that we did. I didn't have the capacity then to conjure up a full parade of horribles, but dim shapes around a greasy fire were enough to set my hairs on end.

As we watched, though, across the field a single flake of fire rose up into the air. From our distant vantage, it was just a speck, like a star falling upwards in bad gravity, but I knew what it was. The fragile paper wings of a crumpled bird, rising and vanishing in the air. I knew that ours had looked the same at this distance.

My father moved from the fire's edge to the border of the darkness. Eyes ahead, he leaned down to probe the shadows, returning with a long, broken branch. The branch's tips were still clotted with leaves, which my father then dipped into our dwindling fire. They smoked, but the flame caught hold and soon gripped the branch in full. My father stood, holding the fiery flag before him like a bright red wing. Then, turning to face our far-off friends, my father began to wave the burning branch—back and forth, back and forth, then pause. Then again.

It felt like hours, but must have only been minutes, because my father's makeshift torch had only just burned itself out when we received a response. There it was, across the field as if in the black mirror of a river light years away. The response, or the perfect mimicry, in flaming semaphore—back and forth, back and forth. Then again. Then nothing.

BIRDS OF PASSAGE

My father was many things over the course of his life, but what he was that night was calm. While images of monsters crowded my head, haunting visions of dark-eyed reflections of a black-eyed father and son waving their flaming lure across the no-man's-land between us, my father remained sanguine.

"Okay," he finally said. "Well, it must be people like us. Probably just passing through." I wanted to believe him, but what gave him away was the stoic deadness to his voice. He was a man of large passions and bold humors, so to hear him modulated was even worse than silence.

Still, through his strength and my own dogged impersonation, we managed to ignore our sister camp for the rest of the evening. We let our fire dwindle and die, and then waited as the one across the field similarly faded from sight. As the night wore on, though, if I borrowed my father's strength to set up camp and eventually crawl into the sleeping bag, then actually falling into sleep was my own weakness. I'm fairly certain that even though he lay down, too, my father never truly slept, because otherwise he wouldn't have been awake when it happened.

"Are you awake?" he asked, but loud enough that it was a question that contained its own answer. It was still thin night, not yet tipping towards morning, and if the sky was a war between black and silver, black was still the clear victor. In fact, as he shook me gently and I first opened my eyes, I wasn't sure it wasn't a dream.

"Are you awake?" he asked again, but he saw that I was because he put his rough palm over my eyes. "Just stay like that," he said, "but you remember where the boat is." It wasn't a question. "If I say so, you go and push off and don't stop, understand?" I nodded by instinct more than awareness, but he must have known, because he said again: "Even if I'm not there, you go alone to the bridge. Do you understand?"

There, beneath the clasp of his hand, I knew that he was serious. I took a moment to let it sink in and visualize myself running from whatever unknown horror lay in the space beyond my father's protection. I could do that, I thought. It would be an adventure.

I nodded.

GORDON B. WHITE

"Okay," he whispered, and drew his hand away. I rose up, though whether on my own or under his power, I can't quite say. I looked out into the distance across the field, expecting to see the neighboring fire rekindled, but instead of illumination all I saw was the roiling dark.

The night itself moved, and the earth itself unrolled.

What at first I had thought to be distant trees moved and swayed, revealing themselves as great long appendages slick with the faint starlight. They towered above us, falling and rising in time to a rhythm that we could not hear. Neither my father nor I could speak to interrupt that moment.

High above, the clouds parted and the bright yellow moon, now full, gazed down on us. Then it rolled its pupil around and the sheer gravity of the thing's attention pinned me to the ground, then slid off me like a wave.

"Does it see us?" I meant to ask, although I don't know if I did or if the way I gripped my father's hand asked for me. But he just shook his head as the giant eye looked away. He hugged me close.

What we saw was awesome, in the truest sense. It was gorgeous and grand and terrible all at once.

It was like the Northern Lights, but of darkest black on a layer of black. It writhed like the coils of giant snakes in the hands of boundless night.

In the distance behind, a mountain shrugged its shoulders and began to move.

And then it was dark again, as if a veil woven of a new kind of darkness had fallen. One that wasn't the absence of things, but rather the richest depths of possibility. A darkness from which anything could emerge.

In the years that followed, I've theorized, but abandoned all theories on what we saw. Something ancient from beneath the earth that sank away again without a trace? An echo of a form on a different dimension, cast like a shadow onto our world? A god? A demon? In the end, I don't know what to call it, but seeing it made me—joyful? In a flash, I had been gifted indisputable proof that there is strangeness in the world that we may never know, but that this universe is an amazing and infinite place. Even if our roles are smaller than we could have ever imagined, to be a part of such a grand machine made me ecstatic.

But even in the twists and turns as my mind re-shaped to accommodate the possibilities of what could be born from the fertile dark, something more tangible emerged. Across the field, two globes of light rose up from the ground. Steadily, they began to move, bobbing and undulating like nodding Cyclopes across the field. My father and I both looked down at our hands to make sure we weren't doing anything that these lights were now mirroring, but no. They were moving on their own.

"Shit," my father said. It was a rare curse that slipped past his lips, as least when I was around. What he did when I wasn't around, however, is something that no one but the dead can answer.

At some point, I suppose, he must have planned what he did next, but I don't know when he could have. Maybe, as you get older, you have a store of actual or imagined experiences to draw from as needed, some stock built up in worries or dreams. Maybe when he thought his son was in danger, there was suddenly a bloom of possibilities that he had seen all at once, as if in a giant knot, and from that he picked the thread that ran out our cord for the rest of our days. All I truly know is that he moved without hesitation.

He picked up a stick and shoved our remaining roll of toilet paper on it. He handed it to me and grabbed another stick, repeating the process with the roll of paper towels. Two sprays of lighter fluid and a light-anywhere match stuck against a rock, and suddenly we both held torches. Although the burst of light blinded me, washing out the rest of the world beyond that blast of illumination, in the distance I could make out giant shadows crawling across the empty fields toward us. The bulbs of their illumination still gleamed even in my swollen eyes, but I wonder what possible horrors or beauties the glare had spared me.

"Wave your torch up and down with me," my father said. We did, like the beating of a bird's broken wings out of unison. Out across the field, although still drawing closer, the iridescent spheres held aloft by the long, dark things did the same.

GORDON B. WHITE

"Run out ten steps, wave it, then run back to me."

I ran, every step away from my father pushing deeper into the viscous night. I waved my flaming beacon and saw him do the same with his.

Across the field, the appendages—for what else could they have been, other than some intelligent part of that great mass?—mimicked our motion. I ran back to my father, the torch swaying up and down as my distant double did the same.

Reunited by the ashes of our dead fire, in our makeshift torchlight, I saw a look in my father's eyes that I had never seen before. I knew love and I knew dedication, but until that moment, I did not know sacrifice.

He grabbed my torch from me and swung them both up and down, up and down. Across the field and drawing closer, the two lights did the same.

"Stay here," Dad whispered. "Close your eyes and count to one hundred. If I'm not back by then"—he nodded towards the river— "you take the canoe. Got it?"

"Yeah," I managed to say.

He smiled. "It's an adventure, isn't it?"

Then he ran, out into the empty field and away from me, swinging the branches of fire like a bird flapping its wings, drawing a path across the dark sky. Across the field, the two lights did the same. They followed him out into the void, towards the wall of the woods on the far side of the field.

I closed my eyes and started counting. Surrounded by the silence, every number in my head was an explosion. At ten I was brave; by twenty I was frightened; I was sucking back tears by thirty. But the night seemed to swallow my sobbing, and by sixty I had stopped. I made it to one hundred, because that's what my father would have done. In part, though, I think I wanted to give it as long as I could, to see what might happen.

Most of what occurred next, I can remember; but all the details are so wound together that even now I lack the perseverance to fully untangle them, so I instead decisively cut through it with only a glance at the pieces. How I opened my eyes in darkness and stumbled over roots back to the banks. How I shoved the canoe out into the black road of the river. How blobs of light seemed to follow me along the shore even as the current pulled me away, fading in the growing dawn until I realized that I was starting at patches of the rising sun coming through branches over the smoking silver ribbon of water.

Hours passed. When I finally got to the bridge, I leapt from the canoe. Feet sucking into the red clay bank, I wrestled the boat up into the switch-thin reeds to wait beneath the very literal and mundane crossroads. Over the hours from grey dawn to robin's-egg blue morning and on to golden noon, my terror ebbed. In its wake, however, I could feel there was a new high-water mark drawn onto my soul—a place where the fantastic had reached up to and left its thin but indelible line. I didn't know then that I might always be searching for that level again, but in the bright light of day—and later, too, even in the darkest night—I knew that there was nothing in this world, or any other, for me to truly fear.

As a result, when the forest wall down beyond the bend began to creak, I again felt that equal mixture of excitement and trepidation. As the skin of the woods trembled, as the knots of branches began to spread, as something emerged, I was open to the full possibility of what might be emerging.

But, still, I was surprised to see my father stumble out of the brambles.

My father, his face ash-grey and his beard much longer than it should have been. My father, staggering beneath some unseen weight, looking gaunt and haunted and as if he was surprised to find himself in the space that he now occupied. He must have seen the canoe or the movement of the weeds, though, because even before I could call out to him, he broke into the closest thing he could manage to a run, bending and tripping through the deep mud and the high grass.

"Gary?" he called out as he approached.

"No," I managed to say. At the sound of my voice, even though every movement was already falling over the top of every other, he moved even faster. He crashed through the last few feet, almost collapsing on top of me, but then wrapping me up in arms that felt thinner than I'd remembered from the night before.

"Is it you?" he asked, pulling me close. "Are you real?"

"Yeah," was all I could say.

He hugged me then, hard, and I'm not ashamed to say I cried. With my face buried in his chest, I could smell the river, but also his sweat and the fire's smoke and something that tingled like if magnets had a smell and you spun them north to south beneath your nose. I never loved anyone more.

"Let's not tell your mom, okay?" he said.

At the time, I thought it was the standard seal of the adventure—that we keep it to ourselves. It was only much later that I realized we wouldn't have been able to adequately describe it. It was better, I now understand, to hold the knowledge of an unlimited world in silence than to make it smaller by trying to explain it.

We only spoke of it once afterwards, years later, when he was in the hospital for the last time. His wife and my sisters were outside talking to a doctor and the whole coterie of aunts and cousins was waiting in the lounge like a conspiracy of ravens, so I was the only one by his bedside when he opened his eyes. I leaned in close, because his throat was parched and his voice was breaking.

"I'm not afraid," he said. He hadn't said what about, but there was really only the one thing—the big Other that hovers over most of us.

"That's good," I said. "Because I might be." I was used to his trailing off by then, and was glad of the silence that bubbled up, but then he spoke again. His eyes got suddenly clear and his voice was strong, like we were back on the river and talking serious man talk again.

"Do you remember Cotner's Creek?"

I nodded.

"I'm glad we were together to see it," he said. "Now, though, there's something else."

"I know."

"I'm not afraid," he said again. The way he looked at me but beyond me, I don't know what he was seeing or if he was fully with me, but it's the only thing that I would give anything not to truly know. Then he said it: "It's an adventure, isn't it?"

He squeezed my hand, his taut sinews closing in like a bird's talons or the long mouths of a school of gar. Then he closed his eyes and fell back into something like sleep. Beneath his thin covering, deep blue rivers of veins pumped slowly along, and I could hear his breath rattling beneath the paper of his skin and in the great empty space behind his ribs.

I never spoke with him again.

As I myself grow older, I often think back to that night on the river. About how there's a world around us, but beyond us, too. A world that takes things, changes them, but sometimes gives them back. All of it—all of it is ripples.

I think back to the flaming wings of paper, rising up and vanishing into the darkness before the thing came to us. Even though my father has since passed on and I, too, am getting old, I have no fear, because I know that in the sky above, in the water below, past that thin thread of night, there are mysteries that we can never know. There is more to it all than you or I could ever fully comprehend and, while that terrifies me, it also brings me comfort.

I know that even if the universe has no thought or regard for our existence, we can give it meaning through our own actions and our love for one another. Instead of hiding in the darkness, we take to wings of flame that bear us on like birds of passage, beating bravely out into the great unknown.

ACKNOWLEDGEMENTS

Starting out writing, especially in horror and the Weird, can feel like typing in a bathysphere. The chatter of the keys reverberates in the tiny iron bubble as great, dark doubts prowl the inky sea just beyond the porthole. When a story's done it goes into a little bottle, then out a little hatch into the abyss with a prayer that it might beat the odds to make it to the surface. Given that, I don't think that I'm unique in feeling an immense pressure to acknowledge every single cable and air hose that has sustained me.

First and foremost, none of this would be possible without my wife, Casey. As my partner in everything for the last eighteen years, she has kept me alive, mostly out of trouble, and provided every kind of support possible. At a close second is our dog, Saucy, but since she doesn't help me proofread, she just barely misses top honors.

I'm also incredibly thankful for my mother, Mary, and my brother, Elliot. They claim to read all my stories, but even if they don't, at least they've learned not to forward them to the more delicate relatives without the once-over.

I've also been fortunate enough to work with a number of talented instructors whose influence and support (and sometimes stories written under their tutelage) can be seen here. I owe a special thanks to Kij Johnson, Gemma Files, Richard Thomas, Sean Hoade, Daryl Gregory, and John Chu.

Writing can be a solitary pursuit, so I must also thank my two adoptive families: Clarion West and The Outer Dark. Clarion West came at an inflection point where I had to decide whether to organize my life around writing or organize my writing around life. My truly heartfelt thanks, then, to the Class of 2017's Adam, Alex, Aliza, Andrea C., Andrea P., David, Elly, Emma, Iori, Izzy, Joanne, Mark, Patrick, Rob, Shweta, Stephanie, and Vina (and you, too, Neile, Huw, and Joe!) for helping me make the call. Go Team Eclipse!

If Clarion West helped me decide how I wanted to organize my life, The Outer Dark, then, helped me do it. I would surely forget too many names to try to list all the creative, kind, and supportive people I've met through them, so I'll have to let it suffice to thank Anya Martin, Scott Nicolay, and their cadre of volunteers for creating this space for a modern and inclusive Weird community.

Despite all that, there have been periods where quitting seemed like the only option, so I owe special consideration to those who offered generous encouragement and/or a kick in the ass when I needed it to get through—especially Clint Smith and Philip Fracassi, although I'll let you guess which was which.

More than any other author, though, I owe a blood debt to my fraternal writing twin, Rebecca J. Allred. We crawled out of the slush together, developing lungs and legs and lists of publications side-by-side. A superb writer in her own right, Rebecca has been a constant beta reader, tireless cheerleader, and confidential shoulder to gripe on.

Thank you, too, to those who made this book a reality: my publisher, Christopher Payne; my editor (and shepherd and hand-holder) Scarlett R. Algee; my proofreader, Sean Leonard; and Don Noble for the fantastic cover.

Finally, I only wish my father, James, was here to read this. Although he's no longer with us, so much of who I am was formed by his family histories, tall tales, and war stories that I feel he's still out there, just above this dark sea, beating wings of fire which leave these pages in the afterglow.

ABOUT THE AUTHOR

Gordon B. White has lived in North Carolina, New York, and the Pacific Northwest. He is a 2017 graduate of the Clarion West Writing Workshop. In addition to writing fiction, he also contributes reviews and interviews to various outlets. You can find him online at www.gordonbwhite.com or on Twitter at @GordonBWhite.